THE SECOND CRASH

Charles D. Ellis Simon and Schuster
NEW YORK

THIS BOOK IS DEDICATED
WITH LOVE AND AFFECTION
TO MY FATHER AND MOTHER,
RAYMOND WALLESER ELLIS AND ELEANOR GWIN ELLIS.
THEY GAVE ME MY VALUES.

FIRST PRINTING
SBN 671-21474-8
Library of Congress Catalog Card Number: 72-93508
Designed by Irving Perkins
Manufactured in the United States of America
By The Book Press, Brattleboro, Vt.

CONTENTS

5

PREFACE

As a student of both the investment business and the securities markets, I have been particularly concerned with the need to resolve the complex and fundamental issues arising from the increasing role of institutions in the marketplace. I have had the opportunity to spend many hours analyzing the problems with leading market makers and senior officers of financial institutions all over the nation, and I believe the time has now come for a major structural change in the way our business is conducted.

The Second Crash describes dramatically how Congress might have written the Securities Act of 1973 *if* in September of 1970, at a time when Wall Street was stretched so terribly thin, Hayden, Stone had failed.

My premise is a simple one: The investing institutions that have full-time, experienced, well-informed, well-equipped professional traders working continuously on the execution of their orders no longer need to have brokers serving as intermediaries between them. The old brokerage system, which worked so well in a bygone era of predominantly individual investors, is both obsolete and dangerous. Moreover, the old system is very expensive. Modifications of this old system may prolong its life, but they will not resolve the basic problems. We need to make the market more properly serve the needs of its primary users—the institutions and the large numbers of individual investors whose savings and investments they manage. To do this, I believe the importance placed on the routine execution of brokerage transactions must be greatly reduced.

All of my proposals have been specifically reviewed by experts. Ideas that I had thought radical have been accepted by men I had thought conservative. While no one has endorsed all of my proposals, none of the proposals has been generally rejected.

The changes proposed are great; they describe a new securities industry. No attempt has been made to modify the reform program to accommodate political or economic realities. These may properly affect the speed with which change is made, but they should not affect the direction of change or the intended objective—which is a clearer sense of the public interest and how the securities industry can best serve it. Getting from here to there will not be easy, but it can be done.

The book is not balanced. It focuses on the problems and the problem makers, and ignores the many able and conscientious people who have done good for the economy and the nation. It shows none of the great affection I have for my colleagues, nor the zest of the money game, which was such great fun while it lasted. The book is deliberately exaggerated for effect. You may find yourself reminded of the mule trainer who was asked if he could handle a particularly cantankerous mule. He said he could make the mule respond simply by whispering into his ear. Then he took a long two-by-four and slammed it across the mule's forehead. "Why did you do that?" the owner asked. The trainer blandly replied, "Because first I need to get his attention." This book hits hard, too, in the hope that its dramatic staging will help all of us see some customary industry practices more clearly and objectively.

Several people generously gave me help in writing this book, for which I am deeply grateful. Susan S. Ellis, as she has in all my writings, gave me a valuable and unusual combination of general encouragement and specific editorial criticism. She's terrific. Jay McDowell, Richard Ramsden, Byron Wien, Lynn Shostack, and Harold Newman each read the manuscript and made many useful suggestions for improving both the logic and the exposition. Sharon Nearier typed and retyped the entire manuscript as an extraordinary gesture of friendship which I'll never forget. William R. Simon has twice been godfather to this book: it was his original idea, and it was he who cajoled me into writing the whole book over again after the entire manuscript and all my notes were lost at John F. Kennedy Airport as Sue, Hal, Chad, and I were returning two years ago from the Bermuda vacation during which the book was originally written. Finally, I am indebted to two talented journalists upon whose carefully researched and detailed articles on the Hayden, Stone difficulties I have heavily relied: Carol Junge Loomis of *Fortune* and Frederick R. Bleakley of *Institutional Investor*. Of course, helpful as these good friends have been, the responsibility of the final text is mine alone.

CHARLES D. ELLIS

Douglaston, New York

INTRODUCTION

ON THE Saturday of the three-day weekend for Lincoln's birthday in 1933, at the request of President Herbert Hoover, the Secretary of the Treasury, Mr. Ogden L. Mills, and the Under Secretary of the Treasury, Mr. Arthur A. Ballantine, went to Detroit, Michigan, to plead with Henry Ford that he subordinate his large-demand account at the Union Commerce Bank.

If Mr. Ford would make this financial concession, a crisis could be avoided. But if he refused, on the Tuesday following Lincoln's birthday that highly leveraged and financially strained bank would fail. And its failure could bring down other Detroit banks, precipitating a banking collapse throughout the state of Michigan, and perhaps even across the entire nation.

During the twenties, banks had been rapidly expanding their activities in stocks and bonds and in long-term home mortgages, both of which had lost considerable portions of their value during the prior three years. The Detroit banks had suffered particularly severe losses because of their exposure to the vicissitudes of the auto industry.

No one denied that banking needed reform, that past abuses and shoddy practices could not be tolerated in the future. But why punish innocent public depositors for the sins of the bankers? A banking panic must be prevented. And now at the eleventh hour only Mr. Ford's personal concession could prevent that panic.

Mr. Ford recognized the character of the predicament. He knew he could step in and prevent panic, but he refused to accede to the urgent requests of Treasury Secretary Mills, saying with moral indignation, "If a panic and crash will come from all this, so be it. Let it come."

The Union Commerce Bank failed Tuesday morning. The other Detroit banks were closed by weekend. During the next month, the panic spread across all of America, and newly inaugurated President Roosevelt was forced to declare a Bank Holiday. Many banks never opened again. Enormous losses were experienced by bankers and by depositors, and the public furor that followed caused Congress to pass a comprehensive program of legislative reforms that changed the structure of the banking industry, redefined the banking business, established vigorous supervisory and regulatory authority, and built strong protections against a future panic. Today America enjoys the advantages of having the world's greatest banking system.

But one must wonder why the reforms could not have been obtained without incurring the awesome costs of that 1933 panic. Unhappily, it is probably true that if Mr. Ford had agreed to cooperate and had saved the banks, few if any of the major reforms would have been enacted. Only the most obvious abuses would have been curtailed.

And today we might still face the risk of a major banking panic and collapse.

This book is about a different panic. A panic in Wall Street. One that didn't happen because, at the moment of crisis, Mr. Jack E. Golsen of Oklahoma City acceded to the pleadings of the high New York Stock Exchange officials. Recognizing that his rejection of their desperate rescue plan would cause a crash in the stock market which would cost too many people too much, Golsen agreed to subordinate his personal financial position to bail out Hayden, Stone at what was almost exactly the last minute. Mr. Golsen didn't have to any more than Mr. Ford had to. Mr. Ford did not; Mr. Golsen did, and that made all the difference.

The fact is there was no crash, that autumn in 1970. Most of the events in this book never happened. But they could have happened. And they very nearly did happen.

Nothing in this book is factual, but it is all true. It tells the truth about the investment community's business morality, its political organization, and its economic structure as it would have been seen by the whole world if the path of history had been only very slightly different. The only change this book makes is that Mr. Golsen, who actually said to Felix Rohatyn, Chairman of the Big Board's Crisis Committee, "O.K., Felix, you've got a deal," is made to say, as he had every right to say, "Sorry Felix, no deal." That is all it would have taken to cause the worst stock market crash in history.

The Crash

Chapter 1 THE PHONE CALL

IN THE end, everything depended on that one phone call

The call was placed at 8:45 in the morning of September 11, 1970, from a small walnut-paneled private inner office that adjoined the formal executive suite of the Chairman of the Board of Governors of the New York Stock Exchange. It was answered in the basement bar and family room of a heavy-construction contractor in Oklahoma City.

The call was made by a small group of powerful men who had recently been charged with responsibility for an *ad hoc* effort to do nothing less than save the Big Board from an approaching disaster. Now, everything they had done in three intensive months and everything they might be able to do in the months ahead depended upon this one call.

Before a full hour had passed, Felix Rohatyn, senior partner in charge of mergers and acquisitions at Lazard

Frères and now serving as Chairman of the Special Surveillance Committee (known more popularly in the Street as the Crisis Committee), and Bernard "Bunny" Lasker, a close personal friend of President Nixon, who was then serving as Chairman of the Board of Governors, had to wrest from Jack E. Golsen of Oklahoma City his immediate acceptance of a complex plan to rescue one of the Exchange's largest firms: Hayden, Stone.

Unless Golsen agreed to go along with the refinancing plan before trading was opened on the Exchange floor at 10:00 A.M. by the traditional clang of an old brass bell, Hayden, Stone would have to be suspended from Exchange membership, would be prohibited from doing business, and the firm would automatically fail. Its failure would bring havoc and panic to Wall Street.

Even if Golsen agreed to the terms of the essential refinancing, there would still be plenty of other major problems that would have to be resolved before the crisis would be over. But if Golsen did not agree now—right now—all the other firms with serious problems would be thrown into immediate, desperate financial trouble and the Crisis Committee would lose all hope of holding back the tidal flood of panic that would inundate Wall Street, bringing a crash more swift and cruel than in '29.

Golsen had every legal right to say "No." He had lent money to Hayden, Stone, and the firm was in default. And he had made his loan on the basis of Stock Exchange data that had since proven false. The representatives of the Exchange had little or no economic incentive to offer to induce him to agree to the refinancing; Golsen believed he would get more of his money back by forcing Hayden, Stone into a financial reorganization. The Crisis Committee had nothing to offer Golsen, and no power to force him to change his mind. All they could do now was plead for some kind of special mercy or appeal to Golsen's sense of the national interest.

For the first time in the history of the Exchange, the leadership found itself hopelessly dependent upon someone who was not even a member of The Club. Lasker and Rohatyn had never met Golsen.

They placed the call anyway. Because they had to. The Exchange and Wall Street, the money center of the Establishment, had less than one hour left.

To understand why that singular telephone call was not merely a quirk of fate, but was instead the culmination of major historical developments in the financial world, we must explore the events that led up to it.

Wall Streeters very much like to style themselves the husbanders of the American Way of Life. They have developed over the years a simple logic in which they believe very deeply. The litany of their belief goes this way: The American Way of Life is Best; America is great because of Democracy; Democracy depends on Free Enterprise; Free Enterprise depends on Capitalism; Capitalism depends on the Central Market; the Central Market is on the floor of the New York Stock Exchange; and therefore, the American Way of Life ultimately depends on the Big Board. Q. E. D.

Outside observers may choose to scoff or smile at this simple concept of the world, but to the members of the Exchange community, all of this is, has been, and always will be True and Just. And for many it is both a business credo and a definition of personal and corporate purpose that fully justifies their enormous incomes and the position of the Big Board, the "core of capitalism," as a unique American business monopoly. The fact is that Wall Street is the only place in America with both fixed prices *and* restricted entry.

Despite its remarkable organization as a business, to analyze Wall Street solely as an economic unit is surely to miss the point. Wall Street is a social organization. And the New York Stock Exchange is its most exclusive Club. The American, or "Curb," Exchange is simply not in the same social class. Those contented but naïve men who say the United States Senate is "the greatest club in the world" simply do not understand what they are saying. Not only has the New York Exchange provided its members with high status in the nation's economy, power in its politics and prominence in its society, it has also made many of its members millionaires and multimillionaires. (And the members' dining room serves the best and most leisurely breakfast that can be eaten in Manhattan.) The Senate may be a very very good club, but it is not the best.

The Exchange is such a fabulous social club that its members almost never had to think of it as a mundane business organization. The profits provided by Exchange membership were so lush, in fact, that most members never had to bother learning how to run their firms as efficient businesses. Who could be bothered with dull operating procedures when money was hanging like bunches of grapes on every vine? Unfortunately, as so often happens, the greatest strength of the Exchange—its ability to generate enormous profits for the members—ultimately became its greatest weakness, because when efficient business management was needed, too many members had no idea how to achieve it.

The Exchange became a powerful club and a weak business organization largely because it was so very much a family business. Even today almost all the firms carry the family names of their principals and founders: Morgan Stanley; Lehman Brothers; Goldman, Sachs; Brown Brothers, Harriman; Kuhn, Loeb; Paine, Webber; etc., etc. (First Boston is obviously not a family name, but then there never were any Uphams in Harris, Upham. Mr. Harris simply adopted his wife's perfectly suitable maiden name when he went into business, to give the firm a sounder image than a single name could provide. And since so many Wall Street daughters have been married to the sons of other firms, most observers have just assumed that Mrs. Harris is a daughter of Mr. Harris' father's partner.)

Wall Street firms were family firms because the families had the capital, and to prosper on the Street a firm must have capital. Capital for clearing brokerage business. Capital for underwritings. Capital for arbitrage. Capital for obtaining swift bank credit. Capital to buy into "lock-ups." Capital for buying into those time-to-time opportunities to make enormous profits on "special situations." But most of all, capital is essential to a firm's standing in Wall Street's social and commercial register because in the final tabulation of status, money is what matters. And money matters very greatly at the corners of Broad and Wall, where, with a slight deference to propriety, money is called capital.

Since brokers and dealers and underwriters think of themselves as capitalists and measure their business successes and failures in terms of capital, they think it is obvious that partners should share in the profits of the firm in proportion to the capital they have contributed to the firm—either individually or as members of the family. The division of profits according to "contributed capital" has been the custom for several generations, and as Ben Franklin correctly observed: "Money begets money."

Men can almost always find mythological explanations for things that seem to work, even when the true explanation is coincidence. As the money partners who were also "family" members prospered mightily and steadily, they came to believe that it was essential for the "good of the economy and the integrity of the central market place" that the world's largest capital market always be financed with the personal fortunes of the partners of member firms.

And who could deny their logic? Certainly experience over the years seemed to confirm their view. For one thing, it was terribly easy to discipline any member who behaved improperly or recklessly because every member could be punished or threatened with punishments that would hurt his own private pocketbook. Discipline was so easy, in fact, that punishments almost never had to be meted out. (The strict application of formal disciplinary rules would have been wholly inappropriate to the informality suited to doing the Club's business.) Besides, the Exchange members were also members of the Families, and formal public procedure is not properly a part of family life and family disputes and family discipline. So an informal leadership circle developed over the years to take care of intramural, interfamilial problems—in private. And while there were formal procedures and titles and office-holders, everyone understood that the real power was exercised discreetly by the "leaders." These informal methods worked so well that only a very few close observers realized that the formal organization of the Exchange was remarkably weak, inexperienced and ill informed, but since this virtually vestigial organization was not needed, its weaknesses were not deemed important.

The reason the Exchange could rely on informal procedures and on the private capital of its individual members was simple: the business was a bore. Readers who think of Wall Street's history in terms of Black Tuesday, the Richard Whitney scandal, J. P. Morgan's mergers, Ivar Kreuger, and Bernard Baruch see excitement, pathos and adventure, whereas in reality ennui and routine prevailed. After all, the Great Crash occurred almost two generations ago, and there are few men in Wall Street today who personally experienced that debacle. Most, by contrast, learned the business during the thirties and forties and fifties when trading volume was low and days with 100,000 shares of total trading (less than 1 percent of today's daily volume) were not unknown; corporations raised only moderate amounts of new capital; interest rates were under 3 percent; and to drum up business, the Exchange went so far as to champion the Monthly Automatic Investment Plan (MIP) for individuals who had as little to invest as $40 every three months.

Wall Street may not have been a bonanza during those long sober years, but it was a good way to make a "decent living" during the week and still have ample time to relax on the weekends. And there was always room for another member of the family in the family firm. It became not uncommon practice for a recent gentleman graduate of Yale or Princeton or even Colgate to be given a seat on the Exchange by a doting grandmother who wanted the boy to join the family firm on the right basis. If he was bright, he might go into the Buying Department, if not he would go into Syndicate or perhaps even down on the Floor. He would then learn the business and make his "decent living."

And if through bad luck in the market or an unfortunate mistake in investment judgment, or even because of attractive, profitable opportunities to expand, the firm needed more capital, it was usually easy enough to raise more capital by visiting wealthy relatives and explaining the proposition in general terms. In fact, the financial strength of Wall Street was not just in the vaults of the member firms. It was in the billiard rooms and on the terraces of the private estates on Long Island. Wall Street could depend, if necessary, on the personal wealth of the families, or what can best be described as "Granny Equity." It was nice to know you could always get money from home if you needed it. Being in the Street during those quiet years seemed as pleasant and unending as a quiet snooze on a summer afternoon.

Calm and prosperity do not prepare people for turbulence and rapid change. Informal organizations are not efficient, nor very effective when facing crisis. And a false sense of assurance and confidence can blur the observer's perception of troubles ahead. The trouble that lay ahead of Wall Street can be summarized in a single word: institutionalization.

And it happened in the sixties. In that one decade, Wall Street went through the kinds of growth and change that most industries had absorbed more gradually over two generations.

Investing is a "people business," and the changes showed up as changes in the kinds of people who came into the business. During the three decades that followed the 1929 crash, most of the young men who went into the Street were scions of the men who were already there. The most ambitious and talented sought careers in Government during the New Deal, they went to war during the forties, and into electronics, marketing and advertising after the war. Law, medicine, management consulting, public service, banking and big business were all clearly preferable to careers in Wall Street, where there were hardly enough opportunities even for the immediate members of the family, and where capital contributions determined the partners' profit participations.

As a result, Wall Street missed an entire generation. And as the older partners in some of the firms took stock of their situations, they concluded that their family heirs were not sufficiently competent and energetic to risk entrusting them, unaided, with the future of the firm on which so much of the whole family's fortune depended. So in the late 1950s they went to the graduate schools of business at Harvard and Columbia and Wharton and Stanford and talked to the MBAs about Opportunity and Promise in Wall Street.

They must have made a reasonably good case, because each year more and more of the ambitious and talented young men went from the business schools into the Street. And at the same time, many of their classmates joined the institutions—the banks, the mutual funds, the investment management firms and the insurance companies—which were growing rapidly in the postwar economic expansion, and were investing more and more money each year in the stock market.

During the early sixties, Wall Street began to recognize the enormous potential profits in doing business with the institutions. After all, when you can execute orders for 200,000 shares of GM for a mutual fund instead of 200 shares for a doctor, and you can charge each customer the same commission for *every hundred shares involved in the trade,* any registered representative can calculate that having one mutual fund account is at least as good as having a thousand doctors.

And since the typical brokerage-firm salesman only keeps 25 percent of the gross commissions, the partners who collect the remaining 75 percent didn't take forever to recognize that getting more institutional business was also very, very lucrative "for the firm." As if to dramatize the magnitude of the opportunity, after three decades during which almost no new firms were formed in Wall Street, dozens of new firms were formed early in the sixties with the specific intention of concentrating exclusively on the institutional customers. Some even refused to have any business dealings with the time-honored individual investor or "retail" customer.

As these new "institutional firms" and the older firms' new "institutional departments" went after the mushrooming institutional commission business, they found that the institutions wanted rather sophisticated services. They wanted in-depth research and expert opinion on all major industries as well as timely insights into smaller growth stocks. So the brokers hired MBAs to be institutional-investment analysts and hired still more MBAs to be institutional salesmen. Wall Street wanted the brightest, most aggressive and ambitious young men because it soon became evident that while the institutions paid brokerage firms little if anything for second-best research or slow-witted institutional salesmen, they paid very, very well for the best.

Those were the glory years for Wall Street. A wealthy individual might have a few million in the market; a big institution had *billions.* Before 1960, a single trade involving 10,000 shares was big news; by the end of the decade, trades would be completed for more than 1,000,000 shares at a time. The largest fund complexes and bank trust departments each were allocating to brokers an extraordinary treasure of $20 and $30 million in brokerage commissions every year. Brokers who would have struggled in 1960 to earn gross commissions of $100,000 found themselves a few years later grossing that amount in a single week and sometimes even in a single day.

And the bright, ambitious MBAs who were producing these bounteous profits from institutional customers knew very well who was getting most of the profits—the partners. So they naturally demanded partnership participations for themselves. When one traditional old-line firm refused to admit "those damned youngsters in the institutional department" into the partnership, those same bright, ambitious young men simply left and formed their own firm—taking much of the firm's profitability with them. And they did not need a lot of capital to earn those profits. Wall Street profits were no longer a function of capital; it was now clearly a service business, and profits depended on talented and ambitious people. They called themselves the New Breed.

Most firms were willing to take into their partnership at least some of the so-called New Breed. But partnerships were still based on capital contributions, and these new people had no fortunes and no "family." Luckily some of the major New York City banks (which are always seeking ways to court the large customer cash balances that brokers keep on deposit at their banks) recognized a unique opportunity to build strong personal relations with the men who would in future years control the major firms (and bank balances) in Wall Street. These enterprising banks agreed to lend the new, unmoneyed partners the cash with which to buy into their firms. (The loans would necessarily be unsecured because of New York Stock Exchange rules against such "capital impairments.") This seemed to solve everybody's needs. The "big producers" in the institutional departments became partners and could now share in the full profits of the firms. The traditional family "money partners" did not have to "carry" the new partners or dilute their capital positions. And the banks had every reason to expect substantial long-term returns on their investments in the Street's future leaders.

On the other hand, it represented a fundamental change in the financial underpinnings of Wall Street, a change whose real significance would not be fully recognized until the end of the decade. As far as the regulatory authorities at the SEC and at the Exchange were concerned, there was no change in the financial positions of the member firms because the new partners were contributing cash to their firms' balance sheets. It looked like a straight equity contribution. And the firms were not making any formal guarantees to the banks on those personal, unsecured loans the banks were making to the new partners. But those were just the appearances and the technicalities.

In truth, it was almost all borrowed money. And while the firm's balance sheet might be "all equity," the new partners' personal balance sheets were "all debts." And that's not all. These new partners had no wealthy relatives out on the Island. They had no Granny Equity. For the first time in two hundred years the firms on Wall Street were becoming solely dependent upon their own resources. They could no longer count on getting extra capital whenever they wanted it. From now on, capital would be limited to what they had in the vaults downtown.

Wall Street was depending more and more upon borrowed money; the Street was becoming leveraged. It wasn't just the bank debts and the evaporation of safe, reliable Granny Equity reserves. There were other kinds of leverage too. Expansion in both retail brokerage and institutional services meant more leased office space, much higher payrolls, and larger and larger computer installations. These were not the highly variable, easily curtailed costs that Wall Street was used to. These cost were fixed.

If business boomed, these fixed costs would "leverage" profits up, up and away. If business turned sour, high fixed costs and large debts would magnify the decline in volume into an acute drop in profits.

But in those glorious days, leverage was not a subject for fear and dread. Leverage was something to seek out and exploit because leverage could make men rich. And Big Leverage could make men Very Rich. And Very Rich is what Wall Street is all about.

So capital in Wall Street firms was not held in cash. Cash can't make money; they called it sterile capital. Instead, it was invested for profits—to make money with money. And by and large it was *not* invested in stocks listed on the Exchange. It was invested in tax-shelter deals to keep partners' income taxes down or in special situations or "lock-ups" or in venture-capital projects that dealt in everything from high technology to mining. It was not safely in the vaults; it was out looking for very big profits. It was not risk-free. And it was not liquid. Wall Street was getting leveraged on a grand scale.

The wonderful thing about leverage is how much it can do *for* you when it works; the awful thing about leverage is how much it can do *to* you when it works against you. And leverage moves faster and farther when it is working against you than when it is working for you—as Wall Street was soon to learn once again. Not only did brokers and brokerage firms become more and more deeply leveraged in terms of their assets and liabilities, but at the very same time, the nature of the operations of the brokers changed substantially and it seemed that every change increased the fixed costs and the amount of capital needed in the business.

The most impressive increase in the need for capital arose from the demands of the mushrooming institutional

investors and the compelling opportunities to profit handsomely by serving those demands. The penultimate
demand of the institutions was for liquidity—the ability
to sell large holdings promptly at or near the current
market price. Institutions don't own one hundred or one
thousand shares of a stock; they own hundreds of thousands of shares. And since every member of the New
York Exchange had agreed that the brokerage commission for transactions should be calculated on a per-
hundred-share basis, with no discounts for large-volume
transactions, everybody went after the buying and selling
being done by the institutions. This was the so-called
block trading business. After all, it was possible to earn a
small fortune doing one good block cross; and most
crosses were set up and done in less than one business
day. (Crossing 250,000 shares meant representing both
the buyer and the seller, so the commission of, say, $30
per 100 shares was earned on 500,000 shares. The total
commission on such a trade would have been $150,000.)

The only problem was that the institutions didn't always fall into line. To be precise, sometimes when one
institution wanted to sell, the brokers couldn't always
find other institutions willing to buy that same stock that
same day at that same price. And other times institutions
were willing to buy, but not as much as the selling institution was determined to sell that day. The block-trading
business was an all-or-nothing business. So if some of the
stock was not purchased, the sale was off. No cross and
no big commission income.

Obviously, something must be done; a solution must be
found—a means to fill the gap on the buy side so the
crosses would take place and those big commission dollars
would come rolling in.

The brokers' only solution was to join in the ranks on

the side of the buyers and use their own money to buy the unbought shares. Their intention was to resell as quickly as possible the shares they had to "position" to facilitate the big-block crosses. And things generally worked quite well. But liquidation of these positions was not always instantaneous; sometimes the positions would take days, even weeks, to resell. In fact, the brokers who were most determined to be important participants in the big leagues of block-trading had to set aside several millions of dollars to be ready to buy blocks whenever institutions wanted to sell blocks. For these firms, millions and millions of dollars were soon absorbed in "positions." And in Wall Street, where most firms have total capital of less than $20 million, a million-dollar allocation of "real money" drawn from the personal fortunes of the partners themselves was a great deal of capital. In many firms, block-trading positions increased the firm's total capital requirements enormously as the firms shifted from being entirely *brokers* with only moderate capital needs and no market-price risk to being also *dealers* with large capital needs and potentially severe market risks. As with all forms of leverage, it was great fun during the bull markets of 1967 and 1968. But it hurt like hell in 1970.

The other enormous need for more and more capital came from the other end of the brokers' client spectrum: the small individual investor. Trading volume continued to expand in the late sixties as the Great Bull Market went into full bloom. Daily volume averaged more than 10,-000,000 shares and reached record volumes of more than 20,000,000 shares in some trading sessions. Of course, all this had been predicted in a Big Board staff study published in 1965. But there was one small hitch—the forecast was ten years off. This volume had been expected in the late 1970s but it came in the late 1960s. Wall Street was not prepared. The needed computers were not yet installed—often they were not even on order. And the old hand process—green eyeshades and all—was simply not up to the task at hand. The old feudal system which had been Wall Street's great strength and power now became a heavy millstone.

Here's why: In retail brokerage, the salesman depends on volume, and to earn a decent living, the salesman has to hustle. He has to go where the action is, working with the stocks that are "acting right," stocks that are "moving" and "breaking out," because these stocks become the popular favorites. And this is what the salesmen sell. And sell and sell and sell. Odd lots, round lots, options, shorts and rapid trading all concentrate in the action stocks.

With good computer-based information-processing capability this would be no problem, particularly if the cumbersome stock certificates did not figure so prominently in the buy-sell transaction. But in Wall Street, every step of every stock transaction requires a clerk to count by hand every certificate involved in the trade. It is difficult for people schooled in the concept of credit cards and a cashless society to appreciate the almost total dependence of Wall Street on the hand delivery, hand receipt, hand checking, hand-delivered return of errors, hand checking of returned certificates, hand redelivery of corrected hand-counted securities, hand count upon receipt, hand count for deposit in vaults until it is time to begin the process all over again because the client has decided to sell.

Wall Street's customary business procedures call for a complete and satisfactory delivery and payment in five business days, and in slow, or even normal, times, this is no trouble at all. But if errors enter into the system, a nightmare of red tape and bustling messengers can rapidly ensue as bundles of certificates are moved back and forth from firm to firm until each attempted delivery is finally made entirely error-free. Errors multiply like fruit flies, and in 1969 errors seemed capable of infinite exponential growth. The result of errors is "fails" (from fail to deliver securities involved in a trade from the seller's broker to the buyer's broker). When this happens, the brokerage firms both settle in cash with their clients and carry a "fail" on their books. Fails are the equivalent of Accounts Receivable in Wall Street.

Any businessman knows that the fastest way to use up your cash is to let Accounts Receivable get out of control. In 1968 and 1969, Wall Street's Accounts Receivable went wildly out of control. Fails got so bad that the Big Board tried to reduce trading volume so fails might be brought back under control by curtailing trading hours. When "short days" were not enough, "short weeks" were tried, with all trading on Wednesdays forbidden. It may have seemed ridiculous to outside observers that the Exchange had to force its members to avoid doing business, but to insiders it was no joke at all to see "fails" soak up their already limited capital with a voracious appetite and also have to forgo commission incomes one day out of five.

A billion dollars is a lot of money, and fails absorbed that amount "going away." Then two billion. Three. Four. Even five billion dollars. And in Wall Street, that was very big money. And this time it wasn't "other people's money." It was firm partners' own capital—which was already in short supply. And it took what had seemed relatively moderate leverage and multiplied it into severe leverage. The heart of the capital markets was running out of capital!

These were serious enough financial problems in a bull

market, but in a bear market they could spell disaster. And the bull market would be over before the 1969 Christmas season.

The bear came on strong. The winter and spring of 1970 saw prices skid at precipitous speed. In Wall Street, it was almost impossible to believe how many things could go wrong—and all at the same time. Volume and revenue dropped badly, but the costs of being in business seemed more fixed than ever before. Block traders found themselves suffering swift losses on position bids—at two hundred and five hundred thousand bucks a crack. And lock-ups that had once been the chance to shoot to the moon became financial nightmares. One firm lost nearly 40 percent of its capital in a single week as prices of the letter stocks in the firm's own account thumped downward. Over-the-counter market makers absorbed quick losses "in size" as unseasoned issues they held in trading inventories were abruptly marked down. At the same time that operating problems were absorbing more and more capital, family fights aggravated by the unusual business pressure of a declining market, deaths of senior partners, retirements, and even "precautionary withdrawals" of capital by inactive family investors cut the supply of capital in Wall Street firms even further. Capital was disappearing like hot water through a wire sieve.

It couldn't have come at a worse time. The capital so sorely needed to conduct the normal business of Wall Street was being removed just as the real need for much larger sums of permanent money was becoming obvious to everyone.

Individual firms tried to solve the problem individually. Wertheim & Co. took in "limited partners" on what amounted to a preferred-stock basis. Salomon Brothers borrowed $20 million privately from a group of institutional investors. The Exchange took "under advisement" the possibility of allowing member firms to raise capital through public offerings of debentures and notes and even appointed a committee to consider this. But as the committee languorously contemplated the philosophical issues, the capital shortage became a serious crunch.

The needs and problems of raising capital publicly were dramatized when Donaldson, Lufkin & Jenrette announced its intention to go public—selling not debt securities, but common stock. The horror with which old-line family firms reacted to the idea of letting every Tom, Dick and Harry buy in—and have ownership rights equal to the senior partners (not to mention letting the smaller firms become major firms virtually overnight by raising relatively enormous sums through stock offerings)—was not really a match for the delight of those who quickly calculated what their own firms might be worth if they could somehow go public, too. Men who had borrowed heavily to buy into firms that were not now as profitable as they had once been could see themselves as instant millionaires. When the Exchange membership finally voted on the issue, history and tradition were given up in favor of the opportunity to get rich—quick.

But it was too late. Like the thirsty mariner, Wall Streeters were unable to dip into the enormous public capital markets that surrounded them. They would have if they could have, but now the bear market was in full force and the operating problems of brokerage firms were legion. In short, the brokers were losing money, or at least they had sharply lower earnings, and were afraid to show a scrutinizing public all that would have to be disclosed in an SEC offering prospectus. They would have to wait, try to weather the storm, and hope to go public another time, perhaps in a year or two. Perhaps never. Meanwhile, the Exchange community, unable to escape the inevitable unfolding of the bear market crunch or even to gain moneyed reinforcements, drifted with a deep and pervasive foreboding into the ultimate battle for the preservation of a centuries-old way of life and business. It was not well prepared.

Part of the reason that danger loomed ahead for many firms was that Wall Street management was not really interested in the operation of the business as a business. Revenues and profits and return on capital were, of course, duly noted and carefully measured. But these are not the real stuff of professional business management. They are only the scoreboard. From an operational point of view, a brokerage firm is—or should be—very much like a bank. Both involve large numbers of routine transactions, and systematic, low-cost efficiency is the key to success. The banks and the brokers were both aggressive recruiters at the business schools in the 1960s, but while the bankers were recruiting men and women for administrative and managerial roles where they could control costs, brokers put their MBAs to work in sales, deals and research, where they could produce revenues, and generally ignored cost controls.

Nor would any self-respecting MBA go into administrative operations at a brokerage firm, where most of his co-workers would be limited to clerical functions, where computers were only grudgingly being introduced, and where the senior operations people had only limited access to the managing partners, and even then had no real influence upon the policies and practices of the firm as a whole. The differences between bankers and brokers could be quickly recognized in the prevailing terminology.

While bankers were referring to their middle management people as Operations Research or Management Information Systems experts, the brokers, who tried to remember to use the term "back office," usually fell back upon the more familiar and colorfully expressive designation "the cage," a term which originated with the wire-mesh protective walls around the cash and securities counting rooms.

The economic and social gulf between the partners' plush and hushed office suites and the noisy and ugly cages was feudal. Caste separation was absolute. Cage people did not come into the partnership and partners did not visit the cage. The partners did not know, and candidly did not care, what was going on in the cage. At least they didn't care so long as everything seemed to be going fairly smoothly.

But then, in the spring of 1970, as fails continued to absorb capital and as operating losses in retail brokerage combined with capital losses in lock-ups, partners in more and more firms began to realize that back office problems, even those not of their own firm's making, could severely hurt them as badly as the offending firms. Because the problems of one firm could quickly become the problem of other firms with whom trades were made, even some of the "inner circle" firms might be in trouble. In other words, the situation was serious. It soon became desperate.

The first real concern came with the failure of McDonnell & Co. The McDonnells were a prominent New York family (the first Mrs. Henry Ford II was one of their daughters). The firm had a good, if undistinguished, record and reputation. It had been expanding its business and had recently brought in Lawrence O'Brien, former Postmaster General and former head of the Democratic Party, to provide professional management for operations and leadership for an emerging national securities firm. But O'Brien resigned in mid-1969 after less than a year. By the following February, the firm's failure and closing were announced to the press. In retrospect it seemed an obvious harbinger, but at the time most observers skipped over it with reminders that "Murray McDonnell had been too stubborn" and suggestions that the internal conflicts and family disputes could have been resolved if he had only been more conciliatory.

Besides, this sort of thing had to be expected. Hadn't the Exchange set up the Special Trust Fund right after the collapse of Ira Haupt & Co. for the specific purpose of providing an orderly means of liquidating firms that failed, thereby protecting the investing public—and Exchange members—from having their securities and receivables tied up during protracted dissolution procedures? There was plenty of money in the Trust Fund to cover McDonnell & Co.'s failure. And besides, one robin does not make a spring. NYSE President Robert Haack telegraphed Senator Edmund Muskie in April that the $25 million Trust Fund was "not near depletion" and that Street finances were vastly improved since early 1969, when Muskie had introduced a broker-dealer insurance bill along the lines of commercial bank deposit insurance by the FDIC. McDonnell was just a special nonrecurring problem—nothing for other firms to worry about. Besides, it was over and done with. Or so they hoped.

But there were other forces at work, and they had important meaning for the Exchange community, even though they were beyond Wall Street control. The Federal Reserve Board of Governors under its new chairman, Arthur F. Burns, was combating inflation and "inflationary expectations" with a vigorous and prolonged tight money policy. With money increasingly scarce, bank loans were hard to get, and so interest rates went up, pushing bond prices down, which in turn pushed stock prices down.

The Fed was intentionally draining liquidity out of the economy. Liquidity is essential to buoyant stock prices, so as the Fed tightened up, the stock market went steadily down. The Fed recognized the high stakes of its policy and in April established a special task force to plan for swift emergency action if, as seemed quite possible, a financial crisis should threaten. In late May of 1970, the stock market seemed to have hit a bottom and had begun to recover. Perhaps the worst was past.

It wasn't. In mid-June, Penn Central called off a major bond issue "for market reasons," and in a matter of days was in bankruptcy. Not only was Penn Central an enormous corporation ("I thought big companies could *always* get more money if they wanted it"), but also it was a major borrower in the commercial paper market where large companies sell short-term debt instruments much as the U.S. Treasury sells Bills. Penn Central's failure could undermine confidence in this very important short term capital market and put many other major companies in a bad cash bind by scaring the buyers of commercial paper into pulling back. A sudden panic in the commercial paper market could be the fuse that would blow up the whole financial system.

Burns moved boldly. He and his *ad hoc* group requested a bank loan guarantee to Penn Central by the Government under a greatly stretched interpretation of the Defense Production Act of World War II. President Nixon, however, vetoed the scheme. Burns's alternative was to work out an informal arrangement with the banks that went like this: When corporations borrow in the commercial paper market, they usually arrange a standby line of credit with their commercial banks in case market conditions make it difficult or too costly to borrow through commercial paper. If Penn Central was unable to pay off its obligations, the commercial paper market would be stunned. More than a few of the companies that depended heavily upon commercial paper, particularly the finance companies that lend to buyers of cars and homes and equipment, would all rush desperately to the banks to get the money they couldn't raise in the distressed commercial paper market. So the banks would have to be ready and willing to lend the needed money or some of those companies would be forced quickly into bankruptcy. And bankruptcies would spread the panic to the stock market. This was no time to risk that.

The solution was simple enough. The banks would lend the needed money promptly upon request to any company having trouble with its commercial paper. But the banks were hard up for cash themselves, and the Fed had been very tough with its questions in recent weeks whenever the banks had tried to borrow extra funds from the central bank. The banks might be reluctant or even unwilling to make these large loans quickly. For Chairman Burns, quick large loans were the only way to solve the problem, so he had all the major banks informally informed over the weekend that they could come to the Fed's discount window and borrow with few if any questions asked as long as the money was for corporations needing cash to pay off maturing commercial paper. The Fed also took the "ceiling" off rates on negotiable Certificates of Deposit so banks could bid in the open market for the funds they would need. It was a bold play and it worked beautifully. But even such an early and decisive move required enormous resources. In less than a month, banks had borrowed one billion dollars from the Fed and another three billion from private investors, setting two records for such an infusion of short-term bank credit.

At the same time that the Board of Governors of the Federal Reserve was rushing $4 billion into action, the Board of Governors of the New York Stock Exchange was slowly dribbling out their $25 million Trust Fund. By April, five member firms had been forced into liquidations that absorbed $17 of the $25 million. And three more firms were moving steadily toward closings that could carry the total requirement to more than twice the money available in the Trust Fund. By July, New York Exchange President Robert Haack was telling Congress that ten Big Board firms were in some form of liquidation. But Haack's official list did not include Hayden, Stone, even though the Exchange had already made an emergency Trust Fund loan of $5 million to that one firm.

Big Board insiders were finding that the biggest problem with weak back-office operations was not that individual firms were losing money from inefficient operations, or that securities thieves were prospering due to sloppy controls, or that partners at more and more firms were losing their personal fortunes. The biggest problem was that the Exchange could not get accurate and timely reports on the financial condition of member firms—even when the Exchange sent in its own auditors. Wall Street was in big trouble, and good information was needed desperately. It was not available.

The whole concept of self-regulation in the securities industry seemed suddenly unworkable just as it was meeting its critical test. The elemental desire for self-preservation, which was so central to Wall Street's system of values and operations, became acute. Brokerage firms are deeply interdependent in their financial operations; the failure of any one firm pulls hard on the solvency of other firms because they are all highly leveraged and the "accounts receivable" of one firm are the "accounts payable" of the other firms. If one firm fails, it will not promptly settle up, and "good receivables" become "fails." Now it became clear that the firms least able to control their own operations and most likely to fail were also the firms least able to provide the Big Board with the factual information needed to protect the general membership from the failures of the few.

New methods had to be employed, and since the Exchange staff had neither the time nor the skills nor the muscle to do the job, Board Chairman Bernard "Bunny" Lasker appointed a special surveillance committee from among the Governors to keep the most deeply troubled member firms from toppling. This group soon became known as the Crisis Committee. Its members included Lasker, Haack, Ralph DeNunzio, Stephen Peck, Solomon Litt and Robert Stott, Sr. This latter-day group worked long hours on hard problems. Its hardest problem was soon recognized to be that of saving Hayden, Stone. And it was Felix Rohatyn, chairman of this group, who would make the fateful telephone call in September.

If all the potential problems of uncontrolled operations and capital impairments seemed to come together all at once into a maelstrom for Wall Street, then the center of the storm was Hayden, Stone. As they say in Hollywood, "It had everything." And everything seemed to be going wrong.

Hayden, Stone had been a reasonably large, reasonably successful, reasonably effective member firm with family management and family capital and a typically diverse line of business. They were brokers, underwriters, investment advisers, and merger and acquisition deal makers. They had lock-ups and venture capital investments. They owned seats on all the different stock and commodity exchanges. They made markets in over-the-counter stocks, traded bonds on occasion, engaged in arbitrage, had a few real-estate deals, distributed mutual funds, did block trades from time to time, and had an institutional research department. They did some institutional brokerage business and had branch offices across the United States and abroad. They helped organize a few hedge funds and developed and sold participations in oil and gas exploration and cattle-raising companies, both of which were intended to provide investors with tax shelters.

And they did all these things without benefit of budgets, long-range plans, management-development programs, cost controls, or modern management information systems. In the management traditions of Wall Street, more was equated with better, and the basic philosophy of management was told in a single word: growth. Not profitability, not control, not consistency: just plain growth. During the 1960s, the firm expanded from 29 to 81 branch offices, had 157,000 customer accounts, more than a thousand salesmen, and gross revenue increased from $23 million in 1960 to almost $125 million in 1968. In retrospect, it is impressive that during Hayden, Stone's very rapid expansion in the mid-60s, it somehow seemed to work pretty well. There was within Hayden, Stone no premonition of the chaos that lay ahead.

Hayden, Stone's first big problem with its operations or "back office" came on the morning of January 26, 1966, when the order room was switched from a manual system to a computer system. It worked for less than half an hour. Then the computer went down. There was no back-up computer, so they tried to switch back to the manual system. But the computer had all the morning's orders trapped inside, and wouldn't dump them out. Clerks and partners scrambled through wastebaskets trying to collect teletype paper copies of orders to piece things back together. Branch office salesmen were screaming for reports on their customers' orders. The debacle lasted three days. It cost Hayden, Stone over $1 million in trading errors. And it hinted at the problems that lay ahead.

In 1968, the firm was continuously losing ground in its operations; errors multiplied, "fails" expanded, and losses and thefts became common. There weren't enough experienced and skilled clerks, and new EDP* systems and OCR† data input subsystems had too many bugs. A brokerage firm, like a bank, must be able to process enormous numbers of transactions quickly, accurately, and efficiently. Hayden, Stone was slow and sloppy. Wall Street wits claimed "You could peel the wallpaper off your wall, deliver it to their cage and get paid $1 million." In a major effort to catch up with the paperwork problems, more and more people from the front office were pressed into service in the cage. It was little help because they didn't know how to do the work that needed to be done. But it did show the ugly severity of the problem when Hayden, Stone's President, Alfred J. "Buddy" Coyle, stayed up all one night trying to help match orders against trade confirmations.

The monstrous magnitude of the problem was shown for the first time when Haskins & Sells conducted the Exchange's mandatory "surprise audit" on August 30, 1968. It took four months to complete and showed that fails-to-deliver totaled $65 million, and that a reserve of $16 million would be needed to cover probable losses from "short differences" (stock certificates that couldn't be found in the safe where they were supposed to be).

* Electronic data processing.
† Optical character recognition.

Setting up that reserve took away 95 percent of the firm's profits. With soaring fails, the firm barely met the required capital-to-liabilities ratio; was compelled to cut back parts of its business; and was finally told to raise $5 million of additional capital by January 1969. Coyle got $4 million. And for a time, the Exchange tolerated the difference.

For Wall Street and for Hayden, Stone, 1969 was a horror. Trading volume fell off sharply. Costs stayed high. Profits shrank and losses expanded. Hayden, Stone lost more than $10 million by the year's end, setting an all-time record.

Then came 1970 and even more severe losses. Even a $5 million tax refund due in March could not keep the firm alive. Then, suddenly, the Big Board, apparently only after strong demands for action by the SEC, demanded that Hayden, Stone increase its capital by $12 million.

Coyle had no place to turn for that kind of money, but maybe Don Stroben, the firm's head of corporate finance and marketing, could get the money. Stroben turned to a group of Oklahoma businessmen whose companies had recently gone public and for whom Hayden, Stone had been the underwriter. They bought the idea, at least in part, because they did not have to put up any cash; they could pledge their own companies' common stocks. And so $18 million of Four Seasons Nursing Centers, CMI Corporation, Woods Corporation, Carousel Products, and LSB Industries were pledged. And after the Exchange "haircut" or discount from current market price, the package of stocks increased Hayden, Stone's capital by the necessary $12 million. For the moment, the firm seemed almost safe.

The crunch came with the spring. In the three months

following the March 13th "Oklahoma rescue," the market dropped sharply, and down went the prices of the Oklahoma stocks. Most of them dropped 50 percent in April and May. Four Seasons was actually suspended from trading and filed for bankruptcy under Chapter XI. The rescue was over; the saviors' big bundle had shrunk to $5 million and Hayden, Stone was again desperate.

Hayden, Stone was almost certainly in violation of the New York Stock Exchange's net capital requirements, but both the firm and the Exchange were unwilling to face up to the problem. By looking the other way on such critical areas as missing stock certificates and by giving generous valuations to the firm's investments, they were able to declare that the ratio of debt to equity was not greater than the maximum allowable 20:1. The SEC might have demanded action except for one critical hitch: What would happen to the firm's many individual customers if, as was more than somewhat suspected, the Special Trust Fund could not cover the losses customers would incur if the firm were suspended? Nobody dared rush things; everybody hoped for a miracle.

Then in June, when another audit from Haskins & Sells showed clear violations of the net capital rule, the Exchange could no longer tuck the problem under a rug, and demanded from Hayden, Stone a definitive plan of action that would overcome the inadequacy. In a final frantic effort to save the firm, Stroben sold stocks and warrants owned by the firm and also the stocks of many of the subordinated lenders who had pledged their shares to collateralize their loans to Hayden, Stone. (Many lenders were shocked when they found out later what had been done to them.) But it was not enough to raise the $11 million they needed.

Then an imaginative solution was proposed to the Exchange. Why not supply some of the needed capital from the Special Trust Fund? The Exchange was at first appalled at the notion. The Trust Fund was to help in *liquidations,* not to finance going concerns. But gradually the idea won acceptance as a temporary stopgap. Besides, the Trust Fund's provisions could be stretched to cover a lot of ground. So the Exchange loaned $5 million to Hayden, Stone, but did not announce its action. What people didn't know couldn't hurt Hayden, Stone, could it?

As it now became clear that it was no longer able to survive on its own, the suggestion was advanced with increased urgency that Hayden, Stone be merged with another firm. They talked to Merrill Lynch; Bache; Reynolds; Shearson, Hammill; and Walston. By August, there was a meeting at the Racquet Club to consider a deal with Walston. The subordinated lenders, whose consent was absolutely essential, and their lawyers were all there. Don Stroben explained the seriousness of the firm's plight. Lee Arning, Vice President of the NYSE, explained that suspension and liquidation of Hayden, Stone was the only real alternative to merger. Almost nobody asked questions or protested. Almost nobody except Jack E. Golsen from Oklahoma City. Golsen did not like the deal. Nor did Larry Hartzog, the lawyer for the Oklahoma group. He wanted a merger with an institutional firm such as Cogan, Berlind, Weill & Levitt, known popularly as CBWL. During the next few weeks, the Walston merger faded away.

By September 3, the lenders were back at the Racquet Club to discuss a very different merger—a takeover by CBWL.* Time was fast running out. This was to be

* Contrary to the narrative in this book, CBWL did in fact take over Hayden, Stone, and the combined firm, which has done very well under the present management, is now known as Hayden, Stone.

Hayden, Stone's only hope. But it would not be easy to obtain consent from a disorganized group of 108 individuals who had made a total of $30 million of subordinated loans to Hayden, Stone in recent years. The problem with them was simple: They would have to agree unanimously to the merger terms, but they were in many cases very independent-minded people.

Even more important, it was evidently the only chance for saving the now fragile structure of the New York Stock Exchange. For those who knew the true facts—very closely guarded secrets—the failure of Hayden, Stone could bring down the entire Big Board.

The reason was simple: Hayden, Stone was not an unusual problem child. Indeed, it was a fairly typical Wall Street firm. And it was one of the five largest firms in the Street. Of the other four, only Merrill Lynch was widely recognized as well managed, efficient, and financially conservative. It could weather almost any storm. The other three were not much more seaworthy than Hayden, Stone.

F. I. duPont had merged with Glore Forgan to form a "superbroker" in the hope of cutting operating costs—but without much success. Moreover, the duPont family, which supplied much of the capital, was not providing strong leadership. Bache was losing money.

And Goodbody & Co., which had had some $65 million in capital in 1969, had seen $20 million withdrawn by partners and subordinated lenders in less than a year and had lost another $20 million from declining stock prices and an operations nightmare, so that only slightly more than a third of its capital remained. And on top of this, an Exchange-required audit showed that a reserve of all or even more than all the remaining capital would have to be set up to make provisions for probable but not yet identified losses due to record-keeping errors—differences between its records and those of its customers and other firms.

In other words, of the five major firms—with more than 2,000,000 customers among them—only one was in good shape. Two were in serious financial trouble and losing their remaining strength rapidly. And the other two were at or near receivership and suspension. One more "downtick" and it would be all over. In fact, it would already have been over except that only an anxious handful of Big Board insiders had even the most general idea of how desperately serious the real situation was. If the situation had been understood, investors would have lost what little confidence they still had, would have sold stocks heavily, and the already weak stock market would have been pushed over the precipice into panic and collapse.

For Rohatyn and his group, the problem was a classic case of the "domino theory"—unless, of course, it all blew up at once because the truth got out before they could somehow overcome the problem one step at a time. Briefly, if Hayden, Stone failed, then Goodbody would fail immediately. This dual failure would surely bring down duPont. And the trio might pull down Bache. In the process, like large boats breaking loose from their moorings at the mouth of a harbor and slamming their way from one small boat to another for the whole length of the haven, the loss of these four majors would take many, perhaps most, of the 1,366 member firms with them. It had happened in banking when Detroit's Union Commerce Bank failed in 1933.

The failure of a large number of important firms in Wall Street would destroy investor confidence and precipitate a cataclysmic panic. With nobody anxious to buy, and many determined to sell, the stock market would crash with a violence that would make 1929 look like a "technical correction." An "institutional" crash would fling down stock prices and threaten the entire capital market—and the savings and security of millions of American families.

The chain of events could even carry dire threats to the nation's balance of payments and the international integrity of the dollar. During the boom of the 1960s bull market, European, Asian and Middle Eastern investors and potentates had bought into the American market through offshore mutual funds, hedge funds, and numbered Swiss bank accounts, partly to make money and partly because America seemed a uniquely stable and safe haven for money. Now even the smell of panic in the Street would cause them to sell out. And the resulting multi-billion-dollar rush away from U.S. securities and the dollar would create an unprecedented strain on international exchange markets and probably even force immediate devaluation of the dollar.

The failure of large numbers of Wall Street's major firms would permanently rend the fabric and organizational structure of the capital markets and the concept of equity investing in America. More than a century of financial leadership by the major brokerage firms and the hegemony of the Big Board would be torn apart. This kind of financial panic could quickly follow the collapse of Hayden, Stone. Hayden, Stone had to be saved.

Saving Hayden, Stone would require a complex refinancing that depended upon convincing CBWL to make a formal offer for Hayden, Stone, and then persuading each and every single one of Hayden, Stone's lenders to agree to CBWL's merger terms. This would not be easy. Any offer to take over this now decrepit brokerage firm would hardly be financially generous. A long series of partial and temporary money-raising deals had left Hayden, Stone with a full 105 subordinated lenders, each of whom would have to agree individually to go along with whatever refinancing offer could be scraped together. To put it more precisely, if any lender said "No," Hayden, Stone was finished. And so was the Big Board.

The essence of the deal finally worked out was simple enough: CBWL would take over Hayden, Stone and combine Hayden, Stone's distribution with CBWL's underwriting organization. CBWL's aggressive management orientation, and their unusually strong and currently underutilized operations capabilities were important advantages. The men from CBWL and the Crisis Committee worked out the details, the essence of which was that CBWL would pay $1 for Hayden, Stone and have the right to sell back to the old Hayden, Stone partnership any branch offices that were not wanted by year end. In addition, CBWL would take Hayden, Stone's cash and marketable securities in exchange for CBWL notes and common stock. Generous? No. But realistic. It might not be ideal, but it was a bid.

So far, so good—but getting the offer accepted would be even harder. The subordinated note holders were scattered all over the globe, and most were tough, independent decision makers. In other words, they could not be herded into an agreement. Each would have to be persuaded on his own terms. And it was already late August. Hayden, Stone would not endure another month. Maybe two weeks, but no longer than that. Time was running out very, very quickly.

By the end of the first week of September, fairly good progress had been made. Most of the note holders were willing to concede defeat and accept the stringent terms offered. (They included the possibility of full payout on the notes only if the combined firm could somehow go public on favorable terms in the future. There were only three holdouts—Donald Eldridge in London, Arthur Rock in San Francisco, and Jack Golsen in Oklahoma City.

In New York, Felix Rohatyn was uncomfortable. Time was working against him. As Lazard Frères' top mergers-and-acquisitions partner, he had always followed the practice of solving the hard parts of negotiations as early as possible rather than holding them for the end, because hard negotiations don't go well under pressure. He demanded and got complete authority to use the Exchange apparatus, individual members of the Board of Governors (and their most prestigious contacts in Washington), and the remaining money in the Special Trust Fund as needed. NYSE President Robert Haack was dispatched on a midnight plane to London and Steve Peck was assigned to bird-dog the San Francisco end. By Thursday, the tenth of September, both teams had won consents, and now all attention focused on Oklahoma City and Jack Golsen, who would play the final card.

The tension mounted in earnest now because an absolute time limit had been established by the execution of an Exchange-sponsored audit of Hayden, Stone which identified in detail a number of items that totaled to "capital inadequacy." They could only be corrected by getting full approval of the refinancing plan, and if they were not corrected before the 10 A.M. bell started trading on Friday, September 11, 1970, under the NYSE Constitution and Bylaws, as approved and enforced by the SEC, Hayden, Stone must be suspended from Big Board membership. The result of such a move would be the immediate failure of Hayden, Stone, and all the havoc and destruction that would ensue.

The Crisis Committee and representatives from CBWL met late Thursday morning to work out a battle plan.

They agreed that a group from CBWL should go out to Oklahoma City that night and meet face to face with Golsen. And if nothing final came out of this meeting, either Lasker or Rohatyn would telephone from New York Friday morning to make a final appeal before the bell opened trading on the floor.

The CBWL team chartered a Lear jet at Teterboro Airport, but bad weather prevented them from taking off until well after midnight. They didn't arrive in Oklahoma City until almost four in the morning. They drove straight to Golsen's home.

The meeting with Golsen was strained. Although both groups were used to being tough, it soon become evident that their worlds were different. They dressed differently. They used different language. Even when they used the same words, they used them differently. Golsen was not used to, and was clearly uncomfortable with, the fixed time limit. In all his previous business dealings, the soundness of the deal was more important than the timing of the final contract signing. But for the CBWL group, with years of experience in block trading and takeover bids, timing had always been a factor and they had learned how to use it. They relished the anxiety and tension; they didn't fight it, they worked with it, trying to force Golsen to make his move.

But Golsen didn't move.

The discussion went on and on. They talked about Wall Street and their plans and their hopes for the newly combined firm and the vital role he would be playing in bringing it all together. But he just didn't buy it. He talked about suing the Exchange and getting his money back. "I'm interested in justice being done here. I want an example made. The only way to bring this awful mess to the attention of the American people is to have a liquidation and let the Exchange and its members lose some real money. Let it all come out and let's clean house."

Nothing they were saying seemed to mean anything to him. Some other approach was needed to get to this guy. Around six in the morning, one of the New York group tried a completely different tack, breaking into the conversation with a "Let's put all our cards on the table right now" tone of voice and said, "OK. Let's call it the way it really is, Golsen. If you don't go along with this refinancing, Wall Street will never ever forget, and you won't be able to raise money or do a deal again for the rest of your life. You need to make this deal as much as we do. You'd damned well better make your move and you'd better do it now."

It was the kind of tension theatrics that had worked time and time again with young institutional portfolio managers who were almost, but not quite, willing to buy a particular block of stock. Push hard. Close the deal. Go for the jugular. But Golsen had been around, and he didn't like being threatened. He simply got up and left the room.

He didn't come back.

Fortunately, his lawyer was able to keep a semblance of dialogue going by moving back and forth between the living room where the CBWL group was sitting and the basement den where Golsen had gone. He understood what would happen if a deal were not made to save Hayden, Stone, and he had hopes that the morning call from Rohatyn might have better results. It was 6:30 A.M. in Oklahoma City, but it was already 8:30 in New York, and the bell would be rung in the balcony high over the trading floor precisely at ten. At 8:45, New York time, the last phone call was placed from Board Chairman Lasker's impressive walnut-paneled formal office at the New York Stock Exchange.

The entire Crisis Committee was there, and the tension was so pervasive that it was agreed that Lasker and Rohatyn should go into Lasker's small private office for their call to Golsen. Rohatyn would talk first, laying out in detail a tough factual statement of the immediate situation, emphasizing to Golsen that there could be no delays or postponements and that there were no alternatives other than suspension or merger with Cogan, Berlind, Weill & Levitt. It would be calm, cold and objective.

Then Lasker would come on and talk very personally and very sincerely about the broad public interest in preserving the central marketplace, the national interest and the tremendous potential hurt to millions of individual investors whose savings were dependent upon common-stock prices. It would be a high-powered one-two punch aiming for a knockout.

As Rohatyn began talking with Golsen, he sensed Golsen's hardened position and his personal antagonism toward the group from CBWL. Golsen complained in blunt terms to Rohatyn that he had lost a lot of money in a very few months because he had relied upon Big Board audits of Hayden, Stone, that these audits had since been proven worthless, and that he didn't see any reason at all why he should now go along with a deal that put him in an even weaker financial position "just so those bastards on the Floor can be saved from their own incompetence and mismanagement." He'd been hurt badly by the Exchange community, so why should he rescue them now?

Rohatyn conceded the irony.

"Irony, hell, Felix, I'm getting clobbered and you know it!"

Rohatyn said he had to agree, but quickly argued that past wrongs could not now be easily righted, that given the present facts, only the takeover offered any real chance of getting Golsen's money back. Something was better than nothing, and nothing was now less than forty-five minutes away.

Golsen was obviously angry, but to Rohatyn he seemed to have accepted the facts of the situation, so he signaled Lasker to start talking on the other extension. Lasker was very effective with his personal, almost intimate, manner and the sincerity with which he pressed Golsen to take a genuinely national view of the decision he was about to make. At twenty minutes before the bell, Lasker put Rohatyn back on the line.

For ITT and other Lazard clients, Rohatyn had negotiated many mergers and acquisitions. Closing was his specialty. Now, in a very few minutes, he had to close with Jack Golsen on the most important negotiation of his life.

Rohatyn was good; he was very good. But Golsen did not say "Yes." When they finished, he had said nothing.

It was 9:45. Golsen said he would call back with a final decision in five minutes.

Rohatyn and Lasker walked back into the main office, where the other members of the Committee had been listening on a speaker phone. Not one word was spoken except by Lasker, who was quietly but urgently instructing the Exchange's switchboard operator to be absolutely certain to hold all calls except one from a Mr. Jack Golsen. Then they just stood there, very much alone— and very much together—and waited for the call from Oklahoma City.

At eleven minutes before ten in the morning, the phone rang. Rohatyn took the call on the speaker phone. It was one of Golsen's lawyers. The emotion in his voice was obvious to everyone in the room. He had been working closely with the Committee for several weeks and had clearly wanted to find a workable solution. He spoke directly.

"Jack says you've got no right to put the squeeze on him again this way. I tried, but he's adamant. Sorry, Felix, but it's no deal."*

* Actually, Mr. Golsen agreed to the terms of the take-over of Hayden, Stone by Cogan, Berlind, Weill & Levitt, and because of his willingness to cooperate, Hayden, Stone was not suspended from membership. Virtually all that follows from this point on is fiction.

Chapter 2 THE CRASH

Rohatyn and Lasker stared at each other in disbelief. "My God, he said 'No'!" The weight of all those long tedious hours of hoping and fearing, cajoling and threatening, talking and talking and talking, that had pressed down around them for so many days and weeks was now nothing. For the moment, the odd euphoria of being briefly in the calm that comes at the eye of the most destructive hurricanes and typhoons held these two men in the silence of that small private office near the top of the Exchange building.

How far detached they were from the normal pre-trading commotion on the floor below them was suddenly very obvious as the door burst open and Steve Peck called them back to the desperate crisis that would be signaled by the 10 A.M. bell.

"Bunny, for Chrissake, we've got to stop the bell. We've got to close down the Exchange or it will all be over."

"It is already over, Steve," said Rohatyn, who was looking at his watch. There was no way to stop trading from opening at the bell in the less than three minutes remaining. "Hayden, Stone is finished. It's too late to do anything about it now."

"Forget Hayden, Stone, Felix. For Chrissake let's save our own necks. We've got to close the Exchange as soon as possible to save as much as we can."

The bell rang to start trading while the seven members of the Committee waited for one of the old open elevators to take them down to the Floor, where they would briefly meet with the Floor Governor as required by the Exchange Constitution and Bylaws, and then they would close the Exchange. It would take nine more minutes.

The news that Hayden, Stone had been suspended hit the Floor like a bomb. The men on the Floor were accustomed to surprise events and it took something really big to rock them. They had been badly shaken by the news of wars and Presidential assassinations, but this was different. This was one of their own. This was one of their leading members. This wasn't just an ordinary bomb. This was a direct hit.

In the nearly ten minutes between the opening bell and the abrupt closing, the Dow Jones Industrial Average lost 87 points. It was a record loss, but it would have been even more of a loss except for the fact that some of the component stocks weren't even opened for trading and so were averaged into the Dow Jones Industrial Average at their Thursday closing prices. (Some amateur statistical experts put the "adjusted loss" of the Dow at 127 points.)

With the early closing that Friday morning, and a weekend coming up, the Governors hoped that Hayden, Stone's failure could be taken more calmly, that most of the danger of panic would subside, and that nothing worse than an orderly retreat in stock prices would be required. Officially, in meetings with the press and in a special interview with Walter Cronkite on CBS, Lasker maintained, as spokesman for the Exchange, that the worst was already over, that Hayden, Stone had been an unusual situation, that its liquidation would be covered out of the Special Trust Fund so no individual investors would be harmed or inconvenienced, and that there was no validity to the "domino theory" for the simple reason that there just weren't any more dominoes. Hayden, Stone was a sad loss, regrettable, but clearly a nonrecurring situation. The other member firms were all sound. There was no reason whatsoever for any lack of public confidence in the Exchange itself.

The Exchange strategy was simple enough. Lasker would say to the world that all was well, the danger was over. At the same time, in the classic tradition of defending against a run on a bank, the Exchange would be open for "business as usual" Monday morning. A sensible play to prevent a local run on a small bank in Charles City, Iowa, perhaps, but in Wall Street it was not good enough. Monday was to be a nightmare.

The professionals at the major investing institutions knew too much. By Sunday afternoon, it was already becoming clear that there must be a lot more trouble than they had thought if Lasker was talking so much like Dr. Pangloss. Everybody knew Goodbody was in real trouble, had already courted merger and had been scorned. It couldn't be said that Hayden, Stone was unique. And Bache and duPont weren't in perfect shape either. Maybe the Exchange was really in trouble. Very big trouble.

Perhaps the trouble would not be very serious after all the smoke cleared, but was it prudent to wait? Maybe this was the time to forget cool and play it chicken, at least for a week or two. This was the time to raise cash, just in case. So sell stocks. Quick. Sell a lot of stock Monday morning.

Every hedge fund, pension fund, mutual fund and bank trust department in the nation had one plan for Monday: Sell. There were no big buyers anywhere.

The opening of trading on Monday was wild. Avon Products lost 18 points on a 350,000-share sale into a position bid from Salomon Brothers. Xerox was off 27 points when 100,000 shares were bought by the Stotts, who were specialists in the stock, but as it continued to drop, they had to close trading. Goldman Sachs and Donaldson Lufkin jointly bid $33 for 400,000 GE—off 10 points. The bid was hit, and before trading was over, the market was $22 bid. It had not been a good bid in that day's market. Each of the two firms had lost $2 million. Avon Products closed at $52, Salomon had lost $5 million. There was no block liquidity left. The ticker tape was more than an hour late at twelve o'clock when once again the Exchange was closed early. Volume was 49,700,000 shares, more than twice the previous record. The average share price dropped $6.26, a little over 20 percent. For the market as a whole, the 20 percent loss was over $150,000,-000,000. One hundred and fifty billion dollars! $150 billion!

During the abortive trading session that Monday, the over-the-counter markets were hit even harder than listed stocks, and as traders dropped their bid prices, they took heavy losses in their trading inventories. In the blizzard of trading volume, costly trading errors also took their toll, and the dreaded fails soared again. The harm was widespread, but it seemed to focus on Goodbody & Co. By the end of Monday's trading, Goodbody no longer met

NYSE net capital requirements. It had to be suspended from membership. Now two of the Big Five were gone. Rumor had it that duPont would be next.

But the worst news was not on the ticker tape; it was on the broad tape, the financial news ticker operated by Dow Jones and supplied to brokers' offices all over the country. In a special bulletin, the Investment Company Institute announced that redemptions of mutual fund shares that morning had been in excess of $500 million, with most of the redemptions being made in aggressive growth funds, particularly a large fund that had specialized in over-the-counter stocks and had large positions in unregistered or "investment letter" stocks and convertible bonds. In other words, even though mutual funds had been heavy sellers in the morning in order to raise cash, they had lost all that cash through redemptions. There would be more heavy selling tomorrow, and with the market collapsing, mutual fund redemptions would be even higher. If it was becoming a run on the funds, they would have to dump stocks wholesale to meet their redemption requirements.

Trouble in the stock market affects other parts of the financial community, too. The banks were much more deeply involved in the stock market than most observers had realized. Commercial banks often accept common stock for collateral against loans, and a group of major banks had financed at least one major corporate take-over attempt by accepting as collateral the shares of the target company bought in the open market prior to a general tender, plus the additional shares obtained in the tender offer itself. The total loan was just under $150 million, and was collateralized with over four million shares of stock. With most take-over loans, the banks get in and get out again in a few weeks. But this tender had been vigorously contested by the target company's management, and not enough shares had been obtained to force a merger. The take-over had been stymied. So the banks had been left on the hook. Now, as the market dropped, the stock collateral under the loan dropped too. By noon on Monday, the four million shares of stock were worth less than the face amount of the loan and the bankers were obliged to call for more margin. They demanded a $30 million partial payment of the loan, but the borrowing conglomerate simply did not have that kind of money on hand. The bankers decided they would have to call the loan, even though it forced the borrower corporation into receivership. So the first major news on the afternoon broad tape was the rumor of bankruptcy proceedings for one of the nation's largest conglomerate corporations, and an intended sale that afternoon of over 4,000,000 shares in a secondary distribution of the target company's common stock. Even in good markets nobody had ever sold anywhere near that much stock in one day. With rapidly dropping stock prices, it obviously was going to be impossible to sell. The banks would have to swallow the loan and a great many other loans like it unless the borrowers could liquidate their collateral. With no big buyers around, nobody was going to be able to liquidate much collateral. Some very big loans to corporations were suddenly in severe jeopardy.

Individuals could receive margin calls as easily as corporations. And they got called for margin on a wholesale scale. Monday afternoon and evening, notices of margin calls went out to over a million customers. Nothing like this had ever happened before. It took most of Tuesday just to complete the mailing out of notices. Tuesday the Exchange was again closed.

The Fed moved in an unprecedented way Wednesday

morning to cut the margin requirement on stock market credit from 80 percent to 40 percent in an attempt to stop the destructive impact of forced sales of stock by individual investors to maintain margin. It was a bold, wise move to protect the market from a credit squeeze, but it made little difference because the real selling was not coming from individuals with margin accounts; it was coming from institutions and they did not need or use margin credit to buy stock so they could not be influenced by stock market credit policy. They bought for cash and they sold for cash. And they were selling with the force of a Panzer blitz.

Foreign investors who had put billions and billions into the American stock market because they had believed that the dollar was the safest currency and that the strength of the U.S. economy and the liquidity of the New York Exchange made American common stocks both safe and rewarding were not favorably impressed by the Fed's action. They were scared—plenty scared.

Suddenly, where there had been confidence there was now doubt. Swiss bankers, Arabian potentates, Greek ship owners and Hong Kong traders moved swiftly to liquidate their holdings. German, French, Italian and English people of moderate means who had invested in the I.O.S. Fund of Funds were not quite so quick, but by Wednesday their redemptions were accelerating rapidly and by the end of trading on Thursday, there was no doubt whatsoever. They were all sellers. The stampede was on.

The run on the funds was becoming a run on the dollar as European banking and financial institutions, assuming that where there was so much smoke there must be fire, and fearing that American insiders probably knew a lot more about the real nature and severity of the American financial problem, simply converted their cash positions from dollars to British Sterling, Swiss Marks and Deutsche Marks.

The Council of Economic Advisers briefed President Nixon Thursday afternoon. They reviewed the nation's basic economic position in some detail and found "no serious problems in the underlying figures" although they took the opportunity to "once again question" the Fed's very tight monetary policy. The problem, they explained, was endemic to the securities market and was not so much a financial or business crisis as it was a crisis of stock market confidence. If confidence could be restored, the problem would resolve itself. It was, they conceded, an important crisis nonetheless. Recent Michigan Survey data indicated disquieting weakness in consumer spending intentions, and the Balance of Payment problem could be seriously aggravated by troubles in the nation's capital markets. And these factors could hurt the Administration's economic programs.

The immediate impact on the stock market was spilling over into other capital markets. Bond prices had slumped badly and commercial paper offerings normally scheduled for the past three days had been reluctantly postponed. The financial markets were in near panic condition and it was not likely that the Fed could again engineer a rescue similar to their Penn Central coup. A stock market-induced recession was very possible, perhaps already probable. In a few days of continued collapse, it would become a certainty. In other words, the Council concluded that the stock market problem was also a political problem.

That night President Nixon addressed the nation on television and radio. He urged calm. He declared himself bullish on America and said he would be buying stocks himself if he had any money to do so. He reviewed the efforts of his administration to brake inflation and hinted broadly at fiscal stimulus to hasten the return to vigorous sales and profit growth. He then announced that with the full support of the SEC and the leadership of the stock exchanges he was declaring a four-day Investors Holiday to give all parties time to consider their future investment needs and opportunities. He concluded with the further announcement that Chairman Burns was marshaling the resources of the Federal Reserve System to prevent the temporary problems of Wall Street from spilling over into other major parts of the financial system.

It was too late. Stock and bond losses and fails and errors during the day had already done irreparable damage to the brokerage firms on Wall Street. In addition to Hayden, Stone and Goodbody, duPont was now closed, and although it was not yet definite, Bache was widely rumored to be insolvent too. Four of the Big Five firms were finished, and the rupture had spread to hundreds of other member firms. Specialists, both weak and strong, regional member firms, regional nonmember firms, and even some of the biggest, most prestigious institutional firms had been forced to close their doors forever.

Manhattan cab drivers were unsure what it all meant. But not the experts in foreign money centers. They knew it meant the time had come to abandon the dollar. Late Friday afternoon, the White House announced that in order to protect the fundamental soundness of the dollar from foreign speculators, the President had directed the Secretary of the Treasury to suspend convertibility and to devalue the dollar by 15 percent.

Stocks were off anywhere from 25 percent to 75 percent. Bonds were off 15 percent to 25 percent. Eleven companies from *Fortune*'s 500 and two banks had been forced into bankruptcy. Nearly 400 member firms had been suspended. Trading volume during the eight hours the Exchange had actually been open had exceeded 100 million shares. Over a million individual brokerage accounts were frozen because of member firm suspensions and bankruptcies. And over $300 billion of market value had been obliterated. On Wall Street it was all over.

The Hearings

Chapter 3 THE EXCHANGE OFFICIALS

THE CRASH hit Wall Street with all the destructive force of a fire storm. Then it was abruptly over, leaving misery and wreckage behind. The heat that caused conflagration in Manhattan would provide Washington with an enormous political barbecue. This would be the biggest and best political issue of the century.

Any really good political issue must involve either scandal in high places or callous treatment of the little man, or money. A politician who could combine two of these three characteristics into a single major issue might construct a campaign theme that would elect him Governor or Senator. The Crash was the penultimate political issue. It had the Eastern Establishment showing disdain for the Public Interests. It had insiders not playing by the Rules of the Game. Smoke-filled rooms and secret deals. Manipulation, prevarication and cheating. Throughout the whole scene ran a single compelling theme: During a period of unprecedented economic growth, high profits and full employment, Wall Street had *independently* produced the most severe and most wide-ranging stock market panic and crash in the history of the free world.

The losses of 30,000,000 common-stock holders; the losses of 40,000,000 indirect investors whose savings were held in pension funds and mutual funds and insurance companies; and the losses of church and college endowments were simply incredible. One economist estimated that the total value of common stocks had fallen from over $800 billion to under $300 billion in less than a year—a total loss of half a trillion dollars. Another savant explained that the nation had lost all the savings of twenty years of hard work; the fabulous fifties and the soaring sixties had suddenly been wiped out.

The more politically dramatic spokesmen pointed out that Wall Street had imposed a "tyrant's tax" five times larger than the entire Federal tax revenues; that the losses were nearly $10,000 for every family in America; that the Crash had cost more than World War I and World War II combined; that Wall Street had thrown away enough money to clean up all the rivers, streams, lakes and ponds in the country; that the lost money could have financed a massive assault on poverty throughout the land. But even these campaign commentaries failed to express the deep, bitter feeling throughout the nation that a great injustice had been done, that the perpetrators must be rooted out and punished, and that a massive rearranging of the financial system was absolutely essential.

Gallup and Harris polls of public opinion showed that Wall Street reform was a better recognized and more provocative political issue than Vietnam, pollution control, the general economy, or social reform. This was indeed such a great political issue that it seemed every candidate for office wanted to get into the act. Happily, it was also such a big issue with so many different worthwhile facets to investigate and legislate about that there was plenty of room for everyone. Almost every American seemed to have a strong personal reason for feeling outraged. When all the individual grievances were totaled up, the Crash made for politics on a grand scale.

Perhaps the clearest evidence of its political magnitude was the remarkable agreement worked out by the Senate and House leadership on the holding of hearings and the drafting of legislation. First, it was agreed that Representative John E. Moss and his House Commerce Subcommittee would be charged with drafting the basic legislation because Moss was recognized as a careful and thoughtful fact-finder with experience in financial affairs who was also a skillful legislative draftsman.

The *quid pro quo* was that the public hearings would be held by the Senate, particularly the so-called investigative hearings that would call as witnesses many of the individuals who had figured prominently in the Crash. Finally, it was agreed that the Senate hearings would be assigned to New Jersey's Harrison Williams and his Senate Subcommittee on Securities when he promised to invite any and all interested Senators to join in his Committee's hearings and to question any witnesses in whom they were particularly interested.

With so many Senators jockeying for position in the 1972 Presidential and Vice Presidential races, the hearings became the major political forum of the decade. Senators Javits, Williams, Percy, Brooke, Bayh, Muskie, Humphrey, Kennedy, Jackson and McGovern all participated actively. (The White House conceded the entire field to the Senate in exchange for an informal understanding that the hearings would not make a spectacle of candidate

Nixon's 1968 letter campaign promise not to "overregulate" the securities industry if he were elected. President Nixon was naturally reluctant to be put on the defensive in public about his real meaning.)

The hearings began in late November and continued through the spring and into the late fall of 1971. The television networks, sensing solid public interest in this unusual daytime drama, formed a special camera pool to broadcast the entire public hearings. Nothing comparable had been seen since the McCarthy-Army episode of the mid-50s. The early tone of the hearings was set by the first witness, Harvard Professor John Kenneth Galbraith, who carefully explained that he could find no real difference in kind—only in scale—between the 1970 crash and the smaller crash of 1929, which he had described in a popular book. Reminding the Senators of the pooling operations, market manipulations, and the ultimate imprisonment of former Big Board President Richard Whitney, Professor Galbraith urged the Senators to be "rigorous, relentless and ruthless in your inquiries and investigations," and emphasized his conviction that major reform legislation was sorely needed.

"We have not seen any major securities regulatory law come out of the Congress in nearly forty years. The world has changed and our capital markets have become obsolete. This is no time for minor adjustments and modifications, gentlemen, this is a time for a complete change. To me, there can be but one answer to the fundamental question with which you must deal. That question is whether our securities laws and regulations should continue to protect the private interests of Wall Street insiders or should henceforth first serve the public interests of the nation's investors."

Major reform legislation in any field was always difficult; the complexity and privacy of the securities field would multiply these difficulties. But even though some Senators might bridle at the hauteur with which Professor Galbraith had assigned them their homework, they all agreed with Senator Williams to continue the investigations until the issues had all been closely examined and the evidence needed for comprehensive legislation had been gathered in. Fortunately, the Committee had a strong staff, and was able to retain a group of economists, brokers, and investment managers who served as experts, guiding the investigators through the Byzantine complexities of the securities business and pointing out the most sensitive and important areas to investigate. Or as Williams once phrased it, "They knew which skeletons were in which closets."

As the Senate hearings continued week after week, it became obvious to all that the structural and procedural problems of the securities industry were enormously complex. It also became clear that the "industry" was so disorganized and had so many conflicting selfish interests involved in every area of potential change that it was wholly unrealistic to hope that the disparate factors in the industry could gain consensus on solutions to any of the major problems. Even if self-regulation had been somehow possible, long before the hearings finally ended the leaders in both the House and the Senate were no longer interested in further reliance on self-regulation. They became convinced that they simply could never again entrust the public interest to Wall Street. Strong Congressional action would be essential.

The hearings began with a general inquiry into the amounts of money lost as a result of the Crash; the impact on the dollar, gold and the balance of payments; the relationship between the market collapse and the bankruptcies of financial and industrial corporations; and the authority or lack of authority of the Securities and Exchange Commission, the Federal Reserve System, the Department of Justice and other agencies of the Federal Government to prevent a recurrence of such a market collapse. Then the hearings were turned toward the New York Stock Exchange and its role in the Crash.

The Senators and their investigators wanted to know how the Exchange was managed. They were surprised to find that because every member of the Exchange held one seat and one vote, the Exchange was controlled not by major brokerage firms but by the so-called floor members —the Specialists and "two-dollar" brokers—who had no direct contact with the investing public, and were not directly supervised by any public or Governmental agency. They were accountable only to the officials of the Exchange, which they themselves controlled. At least that was the way it seemed in testimony before the Williams Committee, which was sometimes clearly antagonistic:

"And so, if I understand you correctly, sir, there is no public disclosure of these Specialists?"

"Well, actually, Senator, we do report the rates of return on invested capital of the Specialist firms each year. So there is disclosure."

"But not on an individual basis. You do not report the volume of trading or the amount of profit earned by each individual Specialist firm, do you?"

"No, we do not. We have felt that such a reporting of an individual member's earnings would be an invasion of his privacy."

"Yet you say he performs a public service. How can you

argue that the Specialist is somehow a public servant in what he does, but can keep private how well he performs his job and how much money he makes each year?"

"We at the Exchange monitor quite closely how well the Specialists perform their jobs, Senator. They do not go unattended."

"But you don't publicly report your findings, do you?"

"No, we do not, although the SEC has full access to our reports."

"Well now, representatives of the SEC have testified before this Committee to the effect that even though they had made strong representations to you and others at the Exchange to discipline bad Specialists, you have been virtually unwilling to do so. That despite numerous complaints the SEC has received from large and small investors about improper practices by Specialists, the Exchange does nothing. Specialists are not fined or reprimanded. Their books on stocks are not reassigned to other more conscientious Specialists. You simply leave them alone, free as can be, to engage when they wish in skimming the cream off the public's transactions."

"Senator, you are condemning with too broad a brush. You are being unfair. Many Specialists make excellent markets. And there is no market anywhere that is the equal of our market. It's the greatest market in the world and the envy of other nations. And it depends upon the Specialists who bring continuity to the auction market system. You are distorting the truth."

"Perhaps. Perhaps not. We have been given detailed factual evidence from the Chairman of the SEC on this matter. He would not agree with you. And his facts and figures would not agree with you. For example, his evidence based on a detailed analysis on a trade-by-trade basis would very much disagree with your views. You say yours is an auction market, but his facts say it is primarily a dealer market instead, and that less than a quarter of all trades are of the auction type. You say the Specialist is essential because he smooths out stock price changes or stabilizes the market, but the Chairman says your Specialists are very often destabilizing and create price fluctuations for their own selfish purposes. And the Chairman also says that his studies at the SEC show very clearly that the bad Specialist—the one who does the *least* to smooth out the market and to make continuous markets— makes almost twice as much profit as the good Specialist makes.

"So don't you come here to the Capital and waste our time and usurp our patience with a lot of fancy abstractions and generalizations. We are conducting these hearings to get the facts. We plan to find out what's been going on up there in New York City and have no interest whatsoever in hearing a lot of public-relations fairy stories."

This was not the only time the Senators would reprimand Exchange officials. They seemed to enjoy embarrassing the Big Board's representatives. For example, they questioned the Exchange executives at considerable length about the seemingly archaic use of stock certificates but only after first hearing from an emissary of the Tokyo Exchange who had explained in detail that his Exchange was able to transact two and three times as much trading volume as the New York Exchange because the Tokyo Exchange had switched from the clumsy certificates to a computer-based central clearinghouse system.

Later, a representative of the FBI testified that thefts of stock certificates had soared into the tens of millions of dollars each year and that stolen securities had become an integral part of the skimming operations of organized crime. Then Williams called to the stand a fat man who was reputed to be a syndicate operative seeking to win amnesty by testifying.

"You are Vincent Charles Teresa, also known as Big Vinnie?"

"Yes, I am."

"And you were personally involved in these thefts of securities?"

"Yes, I was."

"And what part did you play?"

"I was the receiver."

"What is a receiver?"

"I received the securities. Like a fence."

"And where did the securities come from?"

"I dealt mostly with Guarino in New York."

"Is this the man known as Skinny Freddy?"

"Yes, sir, it is."

"And where did he get the securities he brought to you?"

"He had two or three big connections in Wall Street where he got the stocks and bonds. Most of his stuff came from inside jobs."

"And where did the securities go after you handled them?"

"I really don't know. I would mail them to post office box numbers that I was told."

"Who gave you these instructions?"

"I don't know. The instructions were clear and I didn't have to know exactly who was giving me the instructions to know enough to do what I was told."

"Would it have been one Meyer Lansky who gave you these instructions?"

"No. He's too big for that kind of detail."

READER'S NOTE: This seemingly fantastic exchange is based on actual testimony before a Senate Committee.

It was against this background of testimony that the Committee once again questioned the leaders of the Exchange about the paperwork jam-up that forced the Exchange to accept curtailed trading hours in a frantic effort to catch up with the flow of certificates.

"Why do you people at the Exchange continue to have stock certificates?"

"We have a special committee working on ways to reduce or eliminate the role of the physical certificate, but this sort of thing is complex and takes time, Senator."

"And when will they make recommendations?"

"We don't know yet. It takes time to work this sort of thing out."

"How long has the Committee been working on the question?"

"Several years."

The Committee members dwelt at considerable length on the important role stock certificates, particularly missing stock certificates, had played in undermining the solvency of Hayden, Stone and other firms. Under SEC enforced rules, missing certificates or "securities differences" could not be counted as good capital in meeting the capital and liquidity requirements of the Exchange. Several Senators expressed the view that if the Exchange had eliminated certificates when computers had made them obsolete, the Crash might never have had to happen.

Senator Muskie was particularly concerned about the so-called hypothecation agreements under which hundreds of thousands of individual brokerage accounts had been frozen as a result of the suspension or failure of the firms at which these accounts were maintained. His sense of fair play was outraged, he said, when testimony showed that senior partners at many brokerage firms had moved their own stocks and bonds out of their own firms' vaults into safe deposit boxes at neighboring banks so if their firms were suspended, their own funds would not be impounded along with their customers' accounts.

Muskie also probed the rather technical area of free credit balances.

"Will you explain to the Committee, please, just what is a free credit balance?"

"These are the funds left with the brokerage firm, usually when the customer has sold a stock but has not yet reinvested the proceeds."

"And what happens to this money?"

"Under the terms of the typical margin-account hypothecation agreement, these cash balances are commingled with the cash account of the brokerage firm and are then handled together for convenient administration."

"Is it not true that these customer balances are used by the brokers to reduce their bank debts?"

"Yes, that is true."

"And do the customers get paid any interest on these balances?"

"No, they do not because these funds are not a loan by the customer to the member firm. The customer can take the money whenever he wants to. The firm only uses that money on a very temporary basis. So interest is not paid."

"Can you give us any sound reason why these funds should not be fully segregated from the firm's own money?"

"Well, first of all, the amounts involved are usually quite small and very few continue as balances for more than a few weeks. And secondly, the savings on interest expense for the firms is probably passed on to the customers in the form of lower cost and more efficient service."

"If what you say were true, it might make a difference here, but so far, we have had no evidence presented to this Committee that such interest savings are being passed on to the individual customer. All previous testimony says the firms are keeping this secret profit. Do you wish to submit evidence to support your theory at this time? Can you submit any such evidence to this Committee?"

"Not at this time, no, Senator."

"Perhaps you can do so at a later date then, because I remind you, sir, we are not interested in mere hearsay. We want the truth. Now, as to your first point, that these are trivial sums that don't hang around for very long, we have had some strong evidence presented here to the contrary.

"We have had evidence that while the individual cash balances may be transitory and of modest size, the total of such balances is quite large and is virtually constant. To be specific, we have been given factual information

that indicates that nearly half of the profits of several
leading brokerage firms are due specifically to their saving interest costs by using these customer cash balances
as if they were their own. All this makes these balances
seem pretty important."

"Well, Senator, it certainly is a business practice that
has significant economic validity and makes practical
sense."

"I'm sure you feel they should not be changed. That
brokers should continue to have the free and easy use of
these customer monies. Others have been more colorful in
their defense. We've been advised, and I believe I do
quote correctly, that 'It's a matter of life and death for
some firms.'"

The Senators hammered away at the informal nature of
the Exchange's management, the dependence upon committees, part-time executives and awkward methods of
making decisions. They seemed to take particular satisfac-
tion when toward the end of an exhausting four days of
probing the capital inadequacies of member firms, and
the historical reluctance of the Exchange to allow member
firms to obtain permanent-debt or equity financing from
outside sources, the Exchange witness was obliged to admit that in the same year the Board of Governors of the
august New York Stock Exchange had finally ruled that
member firms could raise money by going public, the
Board had also taken formal action to prohibit two common trading-floor practices: water-pistol fights and talcum-
powder showers for recently married members.

Senator Kennedy questioned one former member of the
Board of Governors at great length in what began as

an apparently courtly exchange, but soon showed great animus.

"When you were serving as Governor did you direct the staff to prepare for you a daily listing of all large block trades conducted on the Exchange together with the names of the brokers involved and the names of the institutions involved?"

"Yes, I believe I did. You know, Senator, big-block trading was a relatively new thing for the Exchange in those days and I felt it was my responsibility as Governor to watch this pretty closely in case we should be doing anything about it."

"Did you discuss this information with other members of the Board of Governors?"

"No, I wouldn't do that because this was often pretty sensitive information and had to be treated confidentially."

"Did your duties as Governor absorb all of your time or did you have other responsibilities as well?"

"I was one of the managing partners of my firm at that time, as I have been for many years. And as I hope to continue to be for years to come."

"And isn't your firm a major factor in the block trading business?"

"Well, yes it is. We're quite proud of the unique liquidity we help bring to the central market as a major block trading and positioning house."

"And isn't your own personal background in the trading side of the business?"

"Yes it is, but I don't see what that has to do with my responsibilities as Governor."

"Well, isn't it true that during your term as Governor—

the same period during which you were getting this special information on block trading—your firm's share of the block trading business rose significantly?"

"Senator, we like to think we are a tough and competitive firm, and I surely wouldn't like to say our success depended upon my work as a member of the Board of Governors."

"You might not want to say it, but the facts seem to me to speak very clearly for themselves."

The Committee's Special Counsel picked up the questioning with a vigor that seemed almost excessive to some observers.

"Turning now to another subject, would you personally favor having the so-called supertape on which all transactions on all Exchanges and in the Third Market [listed stocks traded OTC] would be reported to the investing public at the time of the trades?"

"Yes, I support the single-tape concept as an important feature of the central marketplace, and in building investor confidence in that central marketplace."

"But doesn't your statement stand in conflict with evidence we have that during your term as an Exchange Governor, your firm executed more off-board trades, trades not reported on the Exchange's own tape, than were executed by any other firm during this period?"

"Each of these trades involved special circumstances that were fully considered before permission was granted for an off-board execution. Each was approved on its own merits, Senator, by the responsible Governors on the floor."

"You mean your fellow Governors gave you the permission you requested."

During the hearings the Senators returned again and again to the question of self-regulation and whether the concept of self-regulation really was, as Exchange officials claimed, essential to the effective operation of a central marketplace. (Some pundits turned the question around and wondered aloud "whether the central market could endure the consequences of self-regulation.") They were openly skeptical of the ability of the Exchange leadership to escape their "club" and "family firm" antecedents. They were sharply critical of the number and variety of ways in which members of the Exchange community took personal advantage of their quasi-public positions. And they were acutely distressed as a result of their own experience during the spring of 1970 when, months before the Crash, they had been unable to get from the Exchange frank answers to their urgent questions, particularly their questions about the financial solvency of NYSE member firms. The Senators still nursed hard feelings over what they felt had been a deliberate double cross by the Big Board leadership: the Exchange representatives had blandly assured the Senators responsible for drafting the new Securities Investors Protection Insurance Corporation (SIPIC) that the financial problems of the member firms were all over, "just past history," and that no further regulatory controls of the Exchange or its members would be necessary. And then, less than six months later, the Crash had proven the Exchange officials were either woefully misinformed about the financial affairs of their members or, more likely, were deliberately lying.

Senator Muskie, who had been responsible for the

SIPIC legislation, could hardly contain his anger as he questioned the Exchange President.

"Can you tell the members of this Committee why you and the other responsible officials at the New York Stock Exchange kept secret the serious financial troubles of your member firms?"

"We thought it was in the public interest to maintain discretion."

"And why did you deliberately obfuscate the troubles of Hayden, Stone, duPont, and Goodbody?"

"We were trying to act in the public interest as we saw it."

"And why did you and others deliberately and systematically deceive the SEC and members of Congress? Was this also your concept of the public interest? Were you acting secretly and misleading the Government and elected officials and investors throughout this country and even the world, in, as you so glibly say it, the public interest? Oh, no, sir. I put it to you that your mode was not discretion, but stealth; that your means was not disclosure but deception; that your concern was not with the long-term health of our capital markets, but with your own immediate financial position; and that your motivation was not the public interest, but your own private interests.

"Your past actions do very definitely speak louder than your present words. I can assure you that the time has long since passed when either the American people or the Congress of the United States could tolerate your behavior or your attitude. Between the lines of your sanctimonious statements before this Committee, I hear again and again that ugly, intolerable refrain: "The public be damned. The public be damned.'"

Chapter **4** THE BROKERS

As THE Senate hearings continued on into the spring of 1971, the public interest in them—and their political significance—did not fade away, as was so often the case. Instead, the public interest in the hearings grew more intense. Extensive press and TV coverage of the hearings helped, as did the Mike Wallace television specials that explained many of the apparent mysteries of the brokerage and investment-management business. But the main reason for the steady rise in public interest was the growing feeling that Senator Williams' Subcommittee on Securities was on to a serious problem and was doing its job well.

Thus encouraged, hundreds of thousands of citizens wrote long, often anguished, letters to their Congressmen and Senators. (Williams personally received over 4,000 letters in a single day.) Most of the letters involved tales of woe, both real and imagined, of their experiences with retail brokers. In response to this broad concern, Williams scheduled hearings with brokers through most of the spring. The Committee was determined to probe many areas of brokers' activities, but began, in response to obvious public interest, with the problems of an unsophisticated individual investor. In one exchange, the managing partner of a large "wire house" was questioned:

"And what was the size of this widow's portfolio when she came to your firm for investment help?"

"A bit less than $400,000, Senator."

"And how was it invested prior to her coming to your firm?"

"About half was in bonds, with the rest in utility and industrial stocks."

"And how much did she have in her account three years later?"

"Somewhat more than $35,000."

"You mean, sir, that she lost over ninety percent of her money with your firm?"

"This was a most unusual case, Senator. A very unusual case."

"I certainly hope so. Tell me, sir, what action did your firm take in this case?"

"We investigated the account and found that the registered representative with whom she was dealing had obtained full discretion from the customer to make all purchases and sales, and that he had changed her account from a conservative one to a highly aggressive, leveraged trading account."

"You mean he was churning?"

"That is the slang term, yes."

"And after learning these facts, what did you do?"

"We let the salesman go. We dismissed him."

"Nothing more?"

"What more could we do? It was too late to get her money back."

"Well, you might do something to prevent a recurrence, sir. That might be a start."

"We do the best we can to supervise our three thousand salesmen and their five hundred thousand customers, Senator, but you must in fairness remember that this is a very dynamic business and we don't want to overregulate what our clients and salesmen can do."

"I can believe that, because it would hurt your pocketbook to slow trading down. Tell me, sir, just how well do your firm's retail clients do?"

"How do you mean, Senator?"

"Do they make money or lose money?"

"I suppose some lose money, but most, I'm sure, make money with us."

"How much money do they make? For example, do they beat the market?"

"That would be impossible to say, Senator. We haven't made a careful study of that question."

"Perhaps you should. Perhaps the New York Stock Exchange should make such a study. Or perhaps the Congress should appropriate funds for the SEC to make a comprehensive Individual Investor Study and find out just how well or how badly the American people do with retail brokers. There's been a lot of criticism of mutual funds for barely keeping up with market averages. I wonder how well individual investors really do when they, as amateurs, compete against the pros. I suspect they do not do very well. Not well at all.

"Let me make this promise to you, sir: I will introduce legislation authorizing such a study of individual investors and their brokers in the next session of Congress. And I will do so in the hope that some other widow's mite will be saved from this kind of destructive churning. I fully recognize that most of this Committee's attention will be focused on the practices of institutional investors and their impact on the securities industry, but we cannot and will not ignore the unhappy plight of the innocent individual investor who falls into the hands of an incompetent or selfish broker. This kind of churning is far too common, and it must be stopped."

From the potential dangers of churning individual accounts, the Committee turned to a series of reports by staff experts and by consulting economists who had been asked to study the costs and profits of the brokerage business. The SEC's recently completed Institutional Investor Study provided much useful data, and supplemental information was obtained through questionnaires sent to the various Exchanges and to individual brokerage firms.

The evidence was very clear on two points: the brokerage business was very, very lucrative, and while the commission for executing an order for a small individual investor was not very great—averaging only about 1 percent of the money involved—the profit on a large institutional transaction could be very high indeed because the same charge levied on the individual who bought or sold 100 shares was levied on *every* 100 shares of an institutional order even if the institution was trading 500,000 shares.*

Economists pointed out that not only was there no discount for volume buying and selling, but that the bro-

* Some degree of negotiated rates was initiated in April 1971.

ker's costs increased only very slightly as the size of a transaction rose. What was a reasonably profitable business on a retail basis became a bonanza on a wholesale basis. The analysis that impressed the Senators most forcefully was developed by Arthur D. Little and showed that if Big Board trading volume averaged 15 million shares per day (with one buying commission and one selling commission for each share traded) and that if over-the-counter trading plus trading on the American and regional Exchanges was assumed to be equal to the New York Exchange, then the total income to the brokerage industry would be more than $5 *billion* each year.

The Committee was impressed. Even in Washington $5 billion was a lot of money. An awful lot of money.

As broker after broker appeared as witnesses before the Committee, Senator Bayh pressed them to learn where all that money was going. At first, the brokers seemed grateful for the chance to show that they were not keeping all $5 billion for themselves, but it soon became evident that they were playing Brer Rabbit to Senator Bayh's Tar Baby. An economist might say that with fixed prices the brokers were competing for institutional business by increasing their costs—providing more and more services to the institutions to win larger allocations of the total commission pie. An economist might say that, but the investment community had a simpler name. They called it "recip"—reciprocal allocations of brokerage commissions for investment services like research and for noninvestment services of many kinds.

The importance of commissions was partly that they could accumulate to very large amounts over a year's trading at any big institution, partly that they were deducted automatically by brokers and so were not an explicit out-of-pocket expense to institutional clients, and partly that they were as good as cash to the receiving broker.

The testimony on "recip" continued for several days. Here is how the president of a large mutual fund organization explained his firm's position:

"Can you tell the Committee the total annual fees you charge your clients?"

"Our annual investment-management fees are approximately five million dollars per year."

"And what were the brokerage commission costs borne by your clients?"

"These commissions were paid by the funds, not by the individual investors."

"But the investors own the fund, so they paid the commissions even if only indirectly. Now how much were they?"

"On an annual basis?"

"Yes, on an annual basis if you please."

"That would vary depending upon market conditions and upon our investment policy in a particular year, but it would average about fifteen million annually."

"In other words, your clients paid three dollars in hidden charges for every dollar they paid in regular fees?"

"Those are your words, Senator, not mine. You are distorting. Every investor, whether he has his own account with a broker or has his funds in a mutual fund, must pay commissions on each purchase and on each sale. We do not charge him those commissions, the brokers charge them."

"But you use them for your own purposes, don't you?"

"I do not understand your question, Senator."

"Isn't it true that your company selects the brokers with whom you transact purchases and sales for the mutual funds you manage?"

"We do. That is part of our job as investment managers."

"And don't you follow the practice of doing most of this buying and selling with brokers who also sell shares of your mutual funds to the public? Don't you pay out reciprocal brokerage commissions to compensate brokers who do your selling of fund shares for you?"

"That is the custom in the business, Senator. We see nothing wrong with it."

"But isn't this practice now customary for the simple reason that your company can't afford to hire its own sales force and that your customers and prospective customers won't pay an even higher sales load than you now charge? In other words, you depend upon so-called 'recip' to grow and prosper as an investment-management company? And the point is your customers are paying a lot more—two or three times more—to keep you in business than they really believe they are paying. Isn't that the real truth in this situation?"

Reciprocal practices between investment managers and their brokers were not limited to mutual funds. An SEC expert testified to the widespread use of "recip."

"Are you telling this Committee that every financial institution in the country is involved one way or another with mutual back-scratching with brokers?"

"Perhaps not all, Senator, but certainly most institutions are so involved."

"Well, now, we've already had testimony on how mutual fund companies use brokerage commissions on a sweetheart allocation basis to pay off brokers who sell their fund shares. Can you tell us, from your own experience, about the reciprocal practices of life insurance companies?"

"Well, Senator, I know of at least one life insurance company that will make a deal with a broker in which, if he buys his firm's group life insurance or major medical or accident insurance or liability insurance from that insurance company, the company will direct enough brokerage-commission business to that member firm to pay the entire cost of the insurance policy."

"In other words, the broker is getting free insurance?"

"In essence, Senator, yes."

"Is this special dealing done by mutual insurance companies, too?"

"Yes, it is."

"So, if my company is insured by a mutual life insurance company and a brokerage firm is also insured by that company, and theoretically we're supposed to be in it together as equals, in practice my insurance is pretty expensive and his insurance is provided scot-free? Isn't that it in a nutshell?"

"That is essentially the way it works, Senator. Not everybody does it, but many do."

"What about pension funds? Do they play these games too?"

"Well, Senator, some corporate pension funds apparently direct their brokerage business to Wall Street friends and relatives of senior management, say to the

President's son-in-law. And in the area of public pension funds, brokers who do not make generous campaign contributions to local Government officials simply do not see the business. Commissions are money, Senator. They aren't called soft dollars for nothing."

"What about independent investment counselors? Do they get involved in all this?"

"There is a group of brokers, Senator, who hold themselves out as independent experts, who say they will help a wealthy individual or a corporate pension manager select an investment counselor. The wrinkle here is that they have already worked out a prior deal with several investment counselors in which the counselors will pay these brokers, say, four percent in commissions for any money the broker brings in to them."

"So the broker's choice of an investment counselor is not primarily in terms of the investor's needs and objectives or the manager's ability to do the job, but simply in terms of the counselor's willingness to pay commissions to that broker. . . .

"Can you tell us whether banks are in this too?"

"The banks used to be very heavy reciprocators, Senator, but in recent years, they have greatly curtailed this kind of activity, apparently following a Justice Department 'suggestion' to the American Banking Association."

"What practices have banks engaged in?"

"The standard arrangement the banks had would be an exchange of brokerage commissions for compensating demand deposit balances."

"And how would that work?"

"The broker would leave, say, $1,000,000 on deposit with the bank—usually it was money left with the broker, in the form of credit balances, by the broker's retail customers—and the bank would direct its trust-department commissions in the amount of $60,000, if the going rate was six percent, to the cooperating broker."

"And why would the banks do this?"

"Because they could lend the million dollars out at an effective interest rate, after adjusting for compensating balances, of perhaps seven percent or seven and a half percent, and increase their commercial banking profits. In other words, the bankers were in effect recapturing all their trust-department commissions—without having to become Stock Exchange members. For them, it was an ideal setup."

"You make brokerage commissions sound like Green Stamps, with member firms playing the role of the redemption centers."

"That's not an unfair analogy, Senator. Not unfair at all."

"What can you tell us about the regional stock exchanges such as the Boston, Detroit, Pacific Coast, and Philadelphia-Baltimore Exchanges? Where do they fit into this whole picture?"

"Senator, there is a very simple explanation as to why the regional exchanges have flourished. Except for a few local-area stocks that do not qualify for listing on the New York and American Exchanges, most of the business done on the regionals is done in stocks already listed on the two major exchanges. Most of the trading on the regionals is in so-called dually listed stocks and is done by institutions such as insurance companies and mutual funds that are using the regionals for the sole purpose of recapturing their own brokerage business, particularly on the bigger block crosses. If the institutions weren't making big profits in these 'house' commissions, the regionals would dry right up."

"In other words, the regional stock exchanges are

prospering only because they are a device by which the institutions can get a piece of this big, tasty brokerage pie they themselves have created?"

"That is the essence of the situation, Senator. And the same motivating forces are behind the institutions' demands for access to the New York and American Exchanges. They are not trying to cut the costs of brokerage levied on their customers so much as they are trying to increase their profits as management companies. It is a very selfish interest that they pursue."

Some of the hearings on reciprocal commission business were more colorful. One broker conceded that he had bought a small seaplane because he could make a profit by renting it, together with pilot and copilot, to portfolio managers who commuted to Southampton for weekends during the summers. Of course, they paid him not cash, but brokerage commissions.

The brokers seemed in general agreement that the traders working in the order rooms at the institutions were the recipients of unusually generous largess. Tickets to sports events and shows, drinks and dinners in the best restaurants ("I never met a trader who wasn't fat"), and even such favors as color-television sets were all considered routine.

"Have you ever heard of a New York City establishment named Daphne's?"

"I believe I've heard of it."

"And did you personally ever go to Daphne's?"

"I believe I've been there."

"Did you go often, say more than three or four times a month?"

"Yes, I would say so."

"Did you go alone or with guests?"

"I took guests."

"And were these guests usually traders from institutions with whom you hoped to do more brokerage business? And those you took most often paid you the most brokerage?"

"Usually, yes."

"How would you describe Daphne's?"

"It was a club on Lexington Avenue at 92nd Street."

"Don't you mean it was a brothel? A brothel so open in its operation that it had to be closed by the police? It is a sad commentary when brokers have to resort to methods such as this to do business with the nation's fiduciary institutions. Sad indeed."

Another major area of interface between the Street and the institutions was in the area of mergers and acquisitions. Quite often, institutions were the largest stockholders of companies involved in merger negotiations. In such cases, if the institutions voted their shares in favor of the proposed deal, the chances of consummating the deal were greatly increased. And since most investment bankers' fees are at least partially dependent upon a deal going through to completion, the investment bankers assiduously courted the support of the institutions. They arranged special briefing sessions with managements where the expected benefits of the merger would be described in much greater detail than was made available to the general public. And sometimes complete *pro forma* financial statements for the combined companies would be laid out before the cooperating institutional portfolio manager even though such revelations were prohibited under the insider regulations of the SEC.

These coordinated arrangements between investment bankers and institutional investors worked so well that the most aggressive acquisition-oriented conglomerates and their investment bankers began talking to institutions about hypothetical acquisitions even before publicly declaring their intention to take over another company. The practice became known as "warehousing" and was explained to the Committee by an investment banker:

"Warehousing is when a large institutional portfolio manager buys and holds common stock in a company that he knows will soon be the target for a take-over bid. He does this for the sole purpose of making a profit on the stock by selling it to an acquiring company that has promised the institution that it will make the take-over bid for the stock well above the current market."

"And why does the prospective take-over company want to induce institutions to buy and hold these big blocks of stock in the target company?"

"Because the insider rules limit the company that plans to make a tender offer to a ten percent holding in the target company's stock, and a successful take-over depends on the support of large holders."

"And why do the cooperating institutions agree to cooperate?"

"It's an easy way to make twenty to thirty percent on your money in six to nine months because the tender offer is usually that much above the market. And the more stock that is held in friendly hands, the better, because that makes the deal that much surer of going through."

"What institutions engage in this warehousing?"

"All kinds really. Hedge funds, insurance companies, mutual funds and even bank trust departments. It promises instant performance, and among money managers the competition for performance is very intense."

The Committee was concerned to find that the SEC's insider rules did not apply to a group of apparently independent institutions that had banded together with an investment banker to form a pool of like-minded holders of a control block of stock in an unsuspecting company, and that in some cases the investment banker had then literally auctioned off the target company to the highest-bidding conglomerate.

As they got more and more deeply into the nature of the investment-banking business, they became increasingly concerned that the very substantial financial rewards of successful deal-making not only led to improper efforts to consummate mergers and acquisitions but also fostered overzealous selling practices in underwritten offerings of new issues of stocks and bonds. The hearings probed the policies and practices of underwriting firms to determine whether the underwriting firms were offering the investing public sound investment securities or whether, as some observers alleged, the underwriters were more interested in the quantity of these offerings than in their quality.

The inquiry soon focused on the underwriting of securities offerings by the so-called conglomerate companies. The Senate investigators kept coming back to one basic question: If these securities were so very complicated and so very difficult for investors to evaluate and if the prices of many of these new securities had fallen within a year or two to prices that were only 50 percent, 30 percent or even 10 percent of their offering prices, how and why had these corporations been able to sell so many issues for so much money to the investing public? As one wag put it: "Never have so many given so much for so little."

Or, as another, less glib pundit phrased it: "The public was bilked for billions!"

Senate staffers estimated that the total losses in securities offered by conglomerate companies in 1967–1969 exceeded $11 billion, or nearly twice the total amount stolen in all bank robberies since the Revolutionary War.

The Committee soon came to the conclusion that the explanation for the flood of low-grade securities was in the economics of the underwriting business. They found that the key to success as an underwriter was "distribution" capability, the ability of an underwriting firm to sell quickly to its customers the securities it was underwriting. A firm that could move a lot of mechandise would consistently be accorded a preferred position in—a larger share of—each issue. The Senators seemed surprised to find that most issues were essentially presold before the offering became "effective," with the result that underwriters took little, if any, risk on most issues. Senator Brooke observed wryly, "No wonder distribution skill or clout is considered so important."

An aspect of underwriting that seemed particularly puzzling was that while underwriting firms' senior partners always talked in terms of evaluating and appraising the companies whose securities they brought to market, their firms' actual business decisions seemed to be primarily based on the price the securities could be sold at and the profit of participating in the offering. In fact, one investment banker seemed to concede that profit was the only real criterion, explaining: "You have to take your share of the bad merchandise to get your share of the good stuff. Just like in politics, you have to go along to get along."

The Senators kept talking about the investors' money that was lost; the Wall Streeters kept talking about the high principles of their firms and business. Here is part of a typical exchange:

"So, if I understand you rightly, sir, you believe that the most important business decision you and your firm make is whether to associate your firm with a particular underwriting, is that right?"

"No question about it, Senator. The stature and reputation of our firm carries a lot of weight in the financial community and we think we do nothing quite so important as putting our name on an issue."

"You mean putting your name on the offering prospectus as one of the primary underwriters?"

"That's right, Senator."

"Well, just what does this all mean?"

"I'm not sure I follow your thought, Senator."

"Well, for example, how many common stock and convertible security offerings and tender offers and take-over exchange offers did your firm underwrite for Amalgamated Industries during the last five years?"

"Quite a few, Senator. Quite a few."

"Was the total offering price of all these underwritings for Amalgamated as high as $100 million?"

"Somewhat higher than that, I believe, Senator."

"$200 million? $300 million?"

"More than that, actually."

"Wasn't the total more than a billion dollars?"

"It may well have been that high, yes."

"And what is the value of those securities today?"

"That would be hard to say."

"Because Amalgamated is in bankruptcy court, isn't that so?"

"Yes. We are currently advising the Trustees on a program to refinance the company and are hopeful we can work things out."

"And what were your fees as an underwriter of all those offerings? Weren't they well above $50 million? That seems a mighty high fee for helping to drive a major corporation into bankruptcy."

"That is all in the public record, Senator. I don't see what good it does to go into that kind of detail here."

"Then tell me this, sir. What good does it do the investing public to have your firm's name on a bunch of prospectuses when they lose a billion dollars?"

"Risk is a part of the marketplace, Senator. We can't guarantee against risk."

"Then tell me this. While the American people were being bilked for a billion dollars, did your firm ever have to return any part of those fees? Did you suffer any losses when those stocks plummeted?"

"That was not part of our terms of reference."

"You mean that it was OK for the little man to take a lot of risk he probably didn't understand, but your firm, which is one of the largest and most sophisticated on Wall Street, wasn't taking any such risks with your own partners' money? Why shouldn't the enormous rewards of underwriting be balanced with equally heavy penalties so if a deal goes sour, at least the underwriter doesn't get rich while the investors are losing a lot of money?"

It seemed only natural that the Committee pursue the antitrust implications of the underwriting business. A professor from Harvard Business School was one witness.

"Has any major firm gone out of the underwriting business in the postwar period?"

"No."

"Has any major firm lost substantial market share during that period?"

"No."

"Have more than a handful of firms obtained entry into the major underwriting brackets?"

"No."

"Even in competitive bids, is the dealer spread or the price charged by the underwriters ever cut or negotiated? Isn't the underwriting fee fixed before the issue price negotiations even begin?"

"Almost always, yes."

"When new firms don't come into a business and old firms don't get forced out, and prices are fixed, isn't that a classic case of monopoly?"

"Yes."

Several large institutional investors came before the Committee to argue that the Exchange prohibitions against institutional membership were clearly in violation of the antitrust laws, and seemed to make a solid impression with their case for expanding Exchange membership rules so institutions could join, save commission costs, and thus effect savings for their investor customers. The thrust of this argument was countered by Exchange officials who suggested that the real purpose of institutions that sought membership was to keep the saved commissions for the institutional managers rather than to pass them on to their investors. As evidence they pointed to the actual practices of those institutional investors who had joined the so-called regional stock exchanges and generally added all or most "recaptured" commissions to their own profits.

The Committee had rather routinely asked the staff to prepare an analysis of the overall profitability of the brokerage business and had actually expected it to have little importance for these investigative hearings. They were wrong. The study was a bombshell. Contrary to the general impression that brokerage was only a marginally profitable business, the staff study made it look like a veritable cornucopia of profits. The staff analysts were prepared to use econometric and statistical procedures in their presentation to the Committee, but were admonished to keep their analysis as clear and simple as possible. So here is how they did it.

"We assumed the New York Stock Exchange volume would average 15 million shares a day. Of course, this would mean both that much buying and that much selling, so total *commissionable* volume is 30 million shares.

"The average commission is about 30 cents per share, so daily commissions on the Big Board approximate $10 million. With 250 trading days each year, annual commissions totaled about $2.5 billion on that Exchange.

"Since American, regional, and over-the-counter volume is about one-and-one-half times the New York Stock

Exchange's volume, we estimate total commission income of all brokers is between five and seven billion dollars."

"You can't possibly mean that it costs the American people more than $5 billion a year to operate the stock exchanges! Why, that's outrageous!"

"That is the cost, Senator, of brokers' matching orders. It does not include the additional costs of dealers making markets or of underwritings or of market making in Government and corporate bonds. In other words, it is the cost of clearing the market."

"Is there anything comparable, anything to which we can make comparisons, to see how reasonable this cost may be?"

"Senator, we on the Committee staff have only identified one other comparable clearing operation, and that is the clearing of checks among commercial banks through the Federal Reserve System. The Fed's daily volume of checks is about three times greater than the total volume of stock certificates cleared by all stock markets. And, of course, in many ways checks are more difficult to handle because they are often handwritten and because there are many more banks than brokerage firms. Despite these problems, checks are cleared in about one-fifth the time now required to clear stock transactions. Despite these important handicaps, the Federal Reserve System processes its clearing operations for less than $300 million per year, which is about six percent of the brokerage charges to clear stock transactions."

"How is it possible for the banks to perform more transactions more rapidly and more efficiently than the brokers and at a small fraction of the costs?"

"Well, in part it is the incentives. For banks the clearing cost is an expense item while for brokers the commission charge is a revenue or income item. But the main difference appears to be in the technology: banks use sophisticated computers while brokers are only beginning to use computers and still rely on outmoded systems."

"You sound as though you believe the Exchange could be replaced with one big computer."

"Perhaps it is too brief an answer to a complicated problem, Senator, but we met many people who know both computers and the Exchange mechanism, and virtually all of them agree that computers are already capable of providing a more efficient market-clearing facility. The Exchange appears to be a complex process only because men have made it so. The Telephone Company, the Strategic Air Command, NASA and other large-volume information systems could not operate without the advantages of automation. They use computers to process data and to keep the costs down."

"Are computers about to make the New York Stock Exchange obsolete?"

"The Exchange is already obsolete. It is an antique."

"Well, then, given your cost estimates, it is a damned expensive antique!"

Chapter 5   THE INSTITUTIONAL INVESTORS

As THE Senate hearings reopened in the fall of 1971, Committee Chairman Williams scheduled a long series of appearances by officials of the mutual funds, pension funds, banks, insurance companies, investment counselors, hedge funds and endowment funds that had come to dominate the capital markets and the investment business during the past decade. These institutional investors managed billions and billions of dollars of other people's money. As the hearings continued week after week, Scott Fitzgerald's comment, "The very rich are different from you and me," seemed more apt than Hemingway's rejoinder, "Yes. They have more money."

The institutions were very rich. And they were very different from the individual investors who occasionally bought and sold stocks for their own accounts. In some ways, the institutions were simply bigger investors, but in many other ways their activities and needs were very, very different.

Senator Williams was fully aware of the importance of this final phase of the hearings. Not only would this be the first public inquiry into the investment operations of the institutions, but also there had been no major regulatory legislation covering these institutional investors for thirty years. Williams knew Representative Moss was planning to draft reform legislation and didn't want to leave Moss with an open field, particularly such an important one.

Williams took aim at the institutions' participation in the speculative finale of the 1963–68 bull market. It was easy enough to get experts to testify, particularly when the expert was a conservative investor who had been ignored while the press and the public adored the so-called "new breed" of aggressive, performance-oriented fund managers.

One after another, leading traditionalists came before the Committee to help Senator Williams develop a broad indictment of institutionalized speculation.

"In your many years of experience as a professional investment manager, have you found the managers of large institutional investment portfolios engaging in what you yourself would consider speculative practices?"

"In my opinion, Senator, there have been in recent years some very clearly speculative practices by large institutional investors."

"Would you say such speculative investing involved only a small minority of institutional investors?"

"Senator, I'm not really sure how the answer to that question could be quantified explicitly, but in a general sense, I have come to the conclusion that almost all the large financial institutions—and that includes banks, pension funds, endowments, insurance companies, mutual funds and all the others—were involved in one form or another of what any outside observer would have to call speculation. Often they were guilty of speculating in a very big way."

"And what were the practical results of the speculation?"

"Many, many millions and even billions of dollars were lost by investors who didn't know until it was much too late that their savings were being invested in a very speculative way."

"In what kinds of stocks were institutions speculating?"

"Four Seasons Nursing, Minnie Pearl, King Resources, Commonwealth United, Berkey Photo, LTV, Leasco, Data Processing, Parvin/Dohrman, Resorts International, Responsive Environments, Management Assistance and Lums. It's a long, long list, Senator. And a sad one, too."

"Does the Prudent Man Rule apply to these institutions?"

"No, Senator, it doesn't in most cases."

"Is there any reason in your opinion why managers of mutual funds and pension funds and other managers of the invested savings of individual Americans should not be subject to the Prudent Man Rule? Shouldn't every fiduciary be responsible to this basic standard?"

"Senator, I earnestly hope that will become one of the consequences of these hearings. A statement to that effect by the Congress could contribute immeasurably to preventing speculation in future years."

The Committee was particularly interested in the impact of these speculative practices on the individual investor who invested through the institutions rather than directly. Senator Brooke specifically rejected the theory behind the 1933 and 1934 Securities Acts that if the investor was a fool, that was his right, and that regulation should protect him only from manipulative practices and from inadequate disclosure of essential information. Brooke made his point by asking a mutual fund manager whether his fund had invested in LTV, and after being told that the fund had owned over $10,000,000 of various LTV securities, Brooke asked, "Who was responsible for that investment decision?"

"I was."

"Did you study the prospectuses that were issued by the company's underwriters when these securities were offered to you?"

"No, I didn't do that sort of thing. It wouldn't have made good business sense because those prospectuses were terribly long and complicated. I would have had to spend all my time on that one company. We were in regular contact with Street analysts who followed the company closely and kept us posted on the important developments."

"If professionals like yourself don't use them, then what is the real purpose of a prospectus?"

"In theory, it is to disclose all pertinent information that a prudent investor would want to have before making an investment decision."

"Yet in practice, the purpose of a prospectus seems to be to snow the investors rather than to be sure an investor can learn the real nature of the security being offered and the company making the offering.

"Does it help explain matters to present investors with two hundred pages of fine print and financial statements with footnotes that explain footnotes to footnotes? Would you deny that the LTV prospectuses of 1969 and 1970 virtually drenched the investor in disclosure? Would you deny the contention that so much information was presented in such a complex way that few, if any, experts could find their way through them without getting hopelessly lost and confused? And would you deny that such confusion was in fact the real intent of the people who wrote those prospectuses?"

"Senator, there is no doubt that those prospectuses were complex and difficult to digest."

"How many investors do you believe actually studied those prospectuses?"

"I really don't know, Senator. Not many."

"And not even yourself, though you invested millions in that one company. Wouldn't it make sense to have a very brief statement on the first page of each prospectus that states the basic facts of the security being offered in plain English?"

"That might very well help, Senator. It is an interesting idea."

Brooke was not simply suggesting the need to reconsider the purpose of the prospectus. He was trying to show that enormous sums were being invested on behalf of millions of savers, but that almost nobody was taking full and final responsibility for the day-to-day investment decisions. For fund managers to rely on Wall Street analysts for judgments about complex securities, irresponsible as this might seem, was really only part of the larger problem. The theoretical and practical role of so-called independent directors of mutual funds was questioned:

"In addition to your other activities, are you also a member of the board of directors of a large mutual fund?"

"Yes, I am."

"Can you tell the Committee the duties you perform as a director?"

"We meet on a regular basis and have the managers report to us on the investments they hold with particular emphasis on the stocks they have sold or purchased since our last meeting."

"How often do you meet?"

"We meet quarterly, Senator."

"And how long are your meetings?"

"They usually go for an hour or so in the morning and are followed by a luncheon."

"And what are the principal responsibilities of the directors?"

"This varies a bit from fund to fund. We are organized as trusts while some others are corporations. But, in general, we review and approve the investment-management job being done by the managers."

"Don't you also have an important responsibility for approving the contract between the fund and the management company? Don't you negotiate fees and expenses with them and then recommend approval by the shareholders? Aren't you supposed to represent the small shareholders' interests in negotiations with the investment manager?"

"Yes, that is our first concern always."

"But isn't it true that you are selected as a director by the investment manager rather than by the shareholders you are supposed to represent?"

"Well, yes, but that is the custom in the industry."

"But how can you serve as a truly independent director when you know and the management company knows that you were asked by them to join the board of directors because you were their friend and their choice?"

"Just because that's the way directors are chosen, Senator, does not mean we aren't very independent once we join the boards. Let me assure you, Senator, we are very independent directors."

"It seems to me that the ultimate test of the independence you claim for yourself and for all mutual fund directors would be if you ever refused to renew a management contract with your friends, the managers. Do you know of any board of directors of any mutual fund that has asked for competitive bids by outside investment managers who would like to manage the fund?"

"No, I guess not."

"It seems to me that changing managers or some other such independent action by at least one mutual fund's director would do a great deal to resolve the issue now in the courts on whether a mutual fund manager can sell shares to the public or merge his company into another company. If fund directors were really independent, there wouldn't be a lot of these lawsuits about selling and trafficking in fiduciary responsibilities. In the long run such independence by directors might really be in the interests of the fund-management companies themselves. Perhaps directors should be nominated by the fund shareholders instead of by the fund managers. That in itself could help considerably."

The Committee members seemed shocked to learn that individual managers and trustees of some mutual funds were receiving annual compensation in excess of $500,000 each. Senator Muskie suggested that the time had perhaps come for a complete reappraisal of the compensation of mutual fund directors, trustees, and managers, with the specific thought that since the shareholders of mutual funds were, at least in theory, free to negotiate management fees through their director-representatives, perhaps the larger funds should hire their investment staffs to work directly for the funds at normal salaries instead of paying the management companies a fee based on the assets invested in the fund. Muskie was able to show rather impressive cost-reduction opportunities but his "mutualize the mutual funds" idea failed to capture much interest because it was so tame in comparison to the other more sensational subjects covered in the hearings.

Nor was Senator Humphrey able to stir much enthusiasm for his contention that brokerage firms should be paid cash rather than commissions by the institutions for providing investment research. "After all," he pointed out, "whether the manager deducts an openly declared fee or the broker deducts a brokerage commission, the cost is borne by the investor. So why not charge him a single management fee and then, if the manager so wishes, let the manager subcontract—at his own expense—any research he wishes to have done by others?"

The institutional representatives argued that while it was desirable for them to have Wall Street research and they wanted to continue to receive it, they could not afford to pay cash for broker research. Humphrey rejoined: "If you can't afford to pay cash for it, then how can your customers afford to pay cash for it? You may choose to call brokerage commissions 'soft dollars' but that's because you aren't paying them out of your own pocket. You can bet they are very real and very hard dollars—hard-earned and hard-saved dollars—to the investors that you are supposed to be serving!"

Senator Humphrey went on to suggest that one of the

major factors contributing to institutional speculation, both in buying and in selling particular stocks, was that the institutions were all relying on the same sources of information and opinion in Wall Street, and that if broker research were to dry up and each institution were forced to make its own independent investment decisions, the resulting diversity of investment opinion might very well increase the qualities of breadth, depth and liquidity in the market. "In plain words," he asked, "wouldn't the market be a much better market without Wall Street research? Wouldn't we have a better market if investment judgments were independent and diverse instead of centralized, and if the evaluation of securities were divorced from the transactions of purchases and sales? So long as these two elements—value judgments and trading activity—are intertwined in the brokers' compensation, won't the brokers always be more interested in the quantity rather than the quality of buying and selling decisions? Isn't this a classic conflict of interests with the broker interested only in turnover, and the investor interested only in long-term performance?"

Senator Kennedy probed the area of institutional research and got into a classic Wall Street question about who gets called first when an analyst comes up with a hot investment prospect.

"Did you or your firm have any dealings with I.O.S.?"

"I did. And my firm did also."

"As a securities analyst, what was the nature of your relationship with I.O.S.?"

"They were big buyers in U.S. securities and I gave them ideas and factual information on stocks I thought they should buy or sell."

"And they paid for this effort on your part?"

"Yes, they paid me with brokerage commissions directed through my firm."

"Was there anything unusual about the payments you received from I.O.S.?"

"Well, they paid very, very handsomely for good work."

"What was the criterion for evaluating your work?"

"If they made money on my ideas, they made certain I made money, too."

"Did I.O.S. or any representative of I.O.S. ever offer you any unusual incentive to give I.O.S. a special advantage over other investing institutions in the way you supplied information to I.O.S. as opposed to the other clients of your firm?"

"Yes, they offered to pay me $50,000 a year in extra commissions if I would tell them first whenever I thought a stock should be bought or sold and then not tell my firm's other clients until at least a week or ten days later."

"Why would I.O.S. offer these terms to you?"

"Because they could get in or sell out ahead of the institutional crowd."

"And make more money by having this special information?"

"Yes."

Questions about who should be members of the stock exchanges usually involved institutional access, but also got into some interesting sidelights:

"How long have you been the chief executive officer of your company?"

"Twelve years."

"And what is your basic business?"

"We make and sell construction supplies."

"Do you have any other business interests?"

"None that are really significant. Just some invest-ments."

"Isn't it true that you are registered with the National Association of Securities Dealers as the principal in a brokerage firm?"

"That is only a side line, not a major activity, Senator."

"That may be. We shall try to find out. Has your com-pany been active in acquiring other publicly held com-panies in recent years?"

"We've bought a few."

"Have you made tender offers for these companies?"

"In some cases."

"And before announcing your intention to make a take-over bid, don't you usually acquire common stock of the target company, quietly buying as much as ten percent of that company's shares?"

"That is the usual procedure. Our approach is not un-usual."

"But your method is unusual, isn't it? Because you cause the corporation to acquire these shares through the brokerage firm you personally control. Isn't that so?"

"It makes good business sense, Senator. It's the only securities firm we can trust to maintain absolute discretion and secrecy. Besides, the company's directors are fully aware of this situation."

"And the directors are hand-picked by you to go along. Have you disclosed this self-dealing to the stockholders? Do they know where that money is going?"

"That is not required under the law, Senator."

"No, it isn't. But that's why we are holding these hearings—to find out what laws need to be changed. You also have caused your company's pension fund to buy and sell solely through your brokerage firm, haven't you?"

"Senator, my attorney advises me not to answer that question on Constitutional grounds."

"You refuse to answer?"

"I do respectfully decline to answer."

"What is your annual salary from the corporation you say gets the great bulk of your time and attention?"

"The corporation pays me a salary of $135,000."

"And isn't it true that you have received two and three times that amount in profits from your brokerage activities involving the corporation and its business affairs?"

"On advice of counsel, Senator, I respectfully decline to answer that question."

The investment research process was studied at some length with the focus on whether institutional investors were getting an unfair advantage over the individual investors. An executive from a large insurance company testified.

"How many people do you employ in your investment research department?"

"Altogether we have over one hundred people in that area of the company, Senator. It is a large and capable group of whom we are very proud."

"I'm sure you are. Tell us, if you will, how many of these people are responsible for making actual buy and sell recommendations in your insurance company?"

"Approximately twenty-five are what we call senior analysts, and all of them would be expected to recommend purchases and sales for the company to act on."

"And do these men and women try to meet with the managements of the companies they are interested in?"

"Yes, indeed. We believe that is one of their most important duties."

"Why?"

"Because it helps them make better purchase and sale decisions, Senator."

"You mean, sir, that these meetings with top management give them some sort of special inside information?"

"Oh no, Senator, not inside information. But these meetings do provide a solid background in which to interpret current events and factual information that has already been released to the general public."

"In other words, the analyst who goes out to visit top management will be a better analyst than the fellow who doesn't go?"

"Yes, we believe that to be the case."

"Because, if I follow you, sir, the analyst who visits with management will be able to help your company buy stocks lower or sell stocks higher or both."

"That is our responsibility and our purpose, Senator."

"Because your analyst has special access to inside information?"

"That is not the way it works, Senator. We are not after inside information."

"Well, you do expect these trips to be profitable, don't you? Otherwise, why would you spend thousands and thousands of dollars each year sending your best people out to meet with managements? If it weren't profitable, you wouldn't do it, would you?"

"No, of course we wouldn't."

"So it is profitable to meet with management?"

"Yes, it is."

"Well, then, it must be insider information that you're getting because if everybody knew the things your analysts pry out of management, it wouldn't pay to send them out there at all, would it?"

"Senator, you are on a soapbox and you are just burlesquing the idea of insider information. That is not what our people go out for and that is not what they bring back to us."

"Very well, sir, let's drop the inside information terminology because it seems to make you so terribly jumpy. I'm only really interested in the basic principles involved, not the legalistic semantics. Let's see if we can't get down to facts. Now, you say your analysts make better investment decisions if they can visit with management."

"Yes."

"And isn't it true that your analysts like to meet with management in private?"

"Generally, yes."

"And their mission is to help your insurance company make more profitable investment decisions?"

"Yes."

"By buying lower and selling higher than you would without their research and analysis?"

"Yes, that's their role as part of our investment team."

"And you believe they perform that mission better if they meet with top management?"

"We do."

"So when top management meets for a few hours with your analysts, then top management is really helping your analysts make those better decisions, is that not so?"

"In general I would agree with that, but only in a general way."

"But isn't top management supposed to work equally hard for all the shareholders? How can the president or treasurer of a company meet privately with one shareholder and discuss in detail company affairs that are not revealed in full to other investors? Doesn't this necessarily mean that management is helping one shareholder outwit other shareholders? After all, if you sell high, you sell to someone else. And if you buy low, you buy from another stockholder. Should management be helping you buy cheap from other stockholders? Is that management's responsibility? Or shouldn't management treat all stockholders equally and not show favoritism toward the big institutional investor?"

"You are covering a lot of territory, Senator. I can't answer without some simplification or focus to your question."

"Very well, sir. Let me put the question very simply. Is there any proper reason why managements should hold private briefing sessions with selected investors?"

"I think it is rather widely accepted in the investment community, Senator, that if investors are well informed, a company's stock will tend to sell at a higher price and this benefits all shareholders and the company itself."

"Well, then why not have a vigorous effort by management to keep all shareholders fully informed all the time? Under these circumstances, would you still want to have your own special private meetings with management?"

"Yes, I believe we would."

"But other than to outsmart your fellow investors, what would be your reason?"

"That's a tough question to answer without giving it some careful thought."

"Because you really are trying to get special—and improper—inside information, aren't you?"

When Committee members pressed the institutional investors to suggest major structural changes in the securities markets, the institutional representatives invariably argued that the New York and American Stock Exchanges were the best in the world, that the liquidity they provided was essential to the successful operation of institutional portfolios, and that they were in no way interested in becoming Exchange members or brokers provided only that the level of commissions on institutional-sized orders be lowered to a reasonable level in response to the obvious cost efficiencies involved in large-volume trades.

This view seemed entirely logical at first, but as witness followed witness, the Committee members became less and less willing to accept this *prima facie* case on its surface merits. While they fully accepted the excellence of the nation's capital markets in comparison to the markets of other nations, they kept coming back to the high cost of that market. Again and again they came back to one basic question: "Why do you, as professional investors, accept a system of executing orders that costs over $5,000,-000,000? A system in which your fees for making investment judgments and decisions can be exceeded by the brokerage costs of implementing those decisions?"

The institutional representatives offered no solid answers and even conceded that many of the institutions had larger trading operations than the brokerage firms upon whom they relied to carry out their orders. The hearing-room audience was obviously amused by Senator McGovern's suggestion that institutional trading was the only activity outside Government in which there were more people supervising the work than actually doing it.

The hearings covered broad philosophical problems as well as operational matters. The validity of self-regulation was a major concern.

"One of the basic questions this Committee must consider is whether and to what extent self-regulation in the securities industry can and will work. The long tradition of public service and service to individuals in the investment business has been greatly changed by the growth of indirect relationships between investors and their investment advisors due to the emergence of various kinds of institutional investment intermediaries. The investment business is different from what it was ten years ago and perhaps the whole concept of regulation as it applies to that business needs to be drastically updated. A market dominated by institutions—a market in which the institutions do two-thirds of all buying and selling—needs a different kind of regulation. We have had evidence and testimony that the official staff of the Stock Exchange is too short-handed to adequately supervise member firms; that records needed for adequate supervision are not timely, accurate and reliable; that the Exchange leadership treats firms unevenly in disciplinary matters. Even through our own personal experience in the requests this Committee and individual Senators have made for needed information from responsible Exchange officials—requests that were not always met, sometimes were ignored and sometimes met with deliberately misleading statements— the Exchange is not candid with the Congress. This casts a serious pale of doubt over the efficacy of self-regulation, particularly if the objective of that regulation is to serve the public interest. On the evidence, self-regulation is a luxury afforded to the members of the Stock Exchange, a luxury that the public can no longer afford."

"Senator, you should not lose sight of the fact that this country has enjoyed a capital market that is the envy of the entire world because of the speed with which large sums of money can be raised to finance our industrial growth. That, Senator, is the true public interest."

"Quite apart from the question of very high costs of operating this market, costs that nobody has yet tried to justify before this Committee, I do not see the need to have self-regulation in order to have viable securities markets. We have the strongest banking system in the world without self-regulation. We have the best airline system in the world without self-regulation. Our public utilities are not self-regulated. Is there any reason why the securities industry should be the only industry that serves as a public facility that is not regulated? Is there any reason why it would work less well with an independent regulatory agency overseeing the operation of the exchanges and member firms, an agency strong enough in law and in budget to really do the job that is called for?"

No answers were given to this question. And no answers were given to Senator Muskie's question: "Would this market operate any less efficiently if its operating revenues, its brokerage commissions, were cut by thirty percent or fifty percent or seventy-five percent?"

As the Williams Committee wound up its hearings, it was no longer a question of whether substantive reform was needed but rather whether such reform could be achieved during an election year; 1972 was fast approaching and the Senators all recognized that Wall Street was the financial center not only of the nation but also of the Eastern Establishment. How true this was became evident during the hearings.

"While employed by a mutual fund management company did you make any political campaign contributions?"

"Yes, I did."

"In cash or check?"

"In cash."

"Who collected your contribution?"

"A lawyer."

"Did you know him?"

"No, I did not."

"How did you know that he was the person to whom you should make the contribution?"

"I was told that he would come to my office on a particular day and that I should have the money in cash ready for him."

"How much did you contribute?"

"One percent of my salary. The same as other executives in the office."

"And how was this money then used?"

"I do not know precisely, but I was told it would go to Congressmen and Senators who were friends of the mutual fund industry."

"To influence mutual fund legislation?"

"Yes, as I understand it, that was the purpose."

"And were your superiors satisfied with the results of these under-the-counter campaign contributions?"

"I believe they were fully satisfied with the results."

The Senate hearings were unusually long. They were not completed until the spring term of 1972. Some skeptics suggested that the hearings were being stretched out so that Senators could use them as a platform in fulfilling their ambitions for higher office. Others pointed out that while the hearings were somewhat uneven—they covered a unique variety of subject matter—the Committee had held almost continuous hearings and had been well staffed for its inquiry. The job had been done well. By the end, these had been the longest and most wide-ranging hearings in the history of the Senate.

Yet despite the public interest attracted by the Senate hearings, informed observers knew that the future structure of the securities business depended largely upon the quiet efforts of Representative Moss and his House Commerce Subcommittee, which had been meeting almost continuously in a calm, deliberate effort to determine what reforms should be sought and to draft the necessary legislation.

The Legislation

Chapter 6 THE LEGISLATION

WHILE THE prolonged Senate hearings attracted all the attention of the press, television and the public, Representative John Moss and his Subcommittee worked long quiet hours, week after week during the spring and fall of 1971 and into the spring of 1972. Sensing an unusual opportunity to draft important reform legislation, Moss and his dedicated group had agreed early in their deliberations to do their work in private. They refused to discuss their deliberations with any of the many active lobbyists who came from Wall Street and from the institutions to plead for or demand this or that special consideration. They took as their objective the presentation to the Congress of a complete package of reform legislation for the securities industry.

They came to believe that only a truly comprehensive legislative program could deal effectively with the many and varied problems and potential problems that had been uncovered during the Senate hearings and during the Crash itself. Their small Committee was in an extraordinary position to develop an entirely new concept of the securities markets, and they were determined to pursue their reformation without the distractions of pleas from special-interest groups or the disruptive maneuvering of the political process. They felt that if they presented a well-balanced, cogently reasoned, systematic legislative program, Congress might adopt it as a whole and not quibble unnecessarily about specific aspects.

These expectations were well founded because they eventually did succeed in developing a major redefinition of the purpose and organization of the stock market. It promises to be truly landmark legislation.

The real breakthrough in the drafting process came out of Congressman Moss's inability to get a satisfactory answer to a question that kept bothering him: "Why should the operation of the stock market be so doggoned expensive?"

Moss had no difficulty agreeing to the general idea that the strength, size and vitality of the stock market was an important national economic resource and that it should be preserved, but he had great difficulty justifying the actual dollar cost. Quite apart from the question of whether investors made money or lost money, it seemed to Moss that an annual operating cost of between $5 billion and $7 billion dollars (estimates varied and accurate data was not available) was clearly excessive. Why should the annual cost of the stock market's operation be greater than the annual expenditure on space exploration or welfare assistance or foreign aid?

Day after day, Moss kept bringing up this basic question, insisting that in its answer must lie an important key to the legislative puzzle before them. And gradually the other members of the Committee came to agree with Moss that this question did indeed get to the heart of the matter. As they went back and forth over the Senate transcripts, the answer very gradually but very steadily began to clarify in their minds.

Their first major insight was to recognize that while the brokerage business was being investigated and analyzed with great care by economists, statisticians and regulators, they were studying the business from the wrong perspective. They had the wrong frame of reference. They measured the business in terms of individual transactions or trades—how much revenue and how much cost to buy or sell 100 shares of Telephone. That had been an appropriate way to think of the business when it was a retail business. Customers came and went, and each trade had to pay its way. Every tub on its own bottom.

But in the *institutional* brokerage business, two aspects were very different. One was the enormous size of institutional transactions. They bought Telephone in 100,- 000-share blocks and paid commissions 1,000 times larger than 100-share individual investors. The other thing was that institutions were virtually continuous customers and the profit or loss on an individual trade was not nearly so important as the profitability over a long period of time of the business relationship between the institution and the broker. There would be fat years and thin years, easy trades and hard ones, but the nature of the institutional brokerage business was almost completely different from that of the retail brokerage business. The brokers could count on the institutions coming back day after day after day.

The key to the very high cost of the operation of the exchanges was the pricing system, which had almost no discount for volume. (There was a minor discount for very large transactions completed in a single day, but no discounts were allowable for medium-sized trades of, say, 5,000 or 10,000 shares.) Every 100-share unit paid a fixed per unit toll or commission. If the trade involved two units (200 shares), then the customer was charged two tolls. If the trade involved fifty units (5,000 shares), then fifty tolls or commissions were charged. This price structure might have made sense in a field in which volume greatly increased costs but in the brokerage business a trade is a trade is a trade and the cost of doing a 100-share trade is essentially the same as the cost of doing a 100,000-share trade. The same phone calls must be made, the same forms filled out and the same records kept. So while big-ticket trading was not increasing costs, it did enormously increase revenue to the brokers.

And it was in this context that Moss saw the answer to his question. The real function of the Exchange was to *maximize the profits of its member-owners, not to minimize the costs of its users.* And while Exchange officials kept directing the public's attention to the "public interest in having a healthy capital market," the Exchange members directed *their* attention to the profitability of the business.

It was just an enormous put-on. What had the Exchange done to facilitate the raising of equity capital by new young companies? Wasn't it interested only in the large and well-established companies that could obtain new capital relatively easily? And wasn't the profit-maximizing purpose of the Exchange at the root of all the calamitous financial harm suffered during the Crash? How many of the organizational problems and abuses would have developed if the purpose of the Exchange had been efficient, reliable service to users instead of maximum profit to members?

Moss and his Committee decided to try to turn the Exchanges inside out by concentrating on the needs of investors rather than on the profits of members and to see if they could develop a rational system that would not only enhance the long-run vitality of the nation's securities markets, but also achieve their new goal of reducing the costs of the operation of those markets by inventing a new exchange system. It was an ambitious task. And they might never have succeeded if their early deliberations had been subjected to vigorous political debate. But because they were working in private while the Senate hearings attracted the most attention, they had plenty of time and they used it well.

Moss had been wrestling with another question, and its resolution helped point the way for the entire Committee. Moss had wondered why the investing institutions had so readily accepted the pricing structure of the Exchange. Why were they so willing to pay out so much money in commissions? Surely these professional investors knew the approximate costs and revenues of brokers. After all, individuals changed jobs, switching from one side of the Street to the other. So why would a major New York bank pay over $20 million a year for brokerage even though it had more traders in its trading room than most member firms? Why would a group of mutual funds pay $25 million a year to brokers to buy and sell stocks when the fund managers were getting paid less than half that amount to make the decisions?

A Committee member said that to him it almost seemed as though the institutions were working for the brokers rather than the other way around. And then Moss, who is usually a sober, calm, almost somber personality, suddenly clapped his hands in delight and shouted out, "Of course. That's it! By golly, that's it!"

Moss quickly explained his views. The basic structure of the business as it had been practiced was now clear. The institutions had not objected to high commissions (at least not until the end of the sixties bull market) for two very simple reasons. First, the commissions didn't come out of *their* pockets but instead were paid out of their customers' funds. Second, the institutions were deeply involved in exploiting the system *themselves*. Brokers weren't working for institutions and institutions weren't working for brokers. They were working *together*. They were each benefiting from commission abundance.

Moss reminded the Committee members of the several days the Senate had devoted to the question of divorcing investment management from brokerage. The apparent conflicts of interest between brokerage and money management had seemed quite serious. The broker-manager, it was alleged, was interested in higher commissions and higher portfolio turnover, and would consciously or unconsciously do too much buying and selling and so hurt the investment performance of client portfolios. It had seemed an ideal issue, but as the Senate Committee called witness after witness, it had become clear that the potential problems were so easily recognized and of such concern to both clients and brokers that, in almost every case, they had found a sensible solution. Significantly, the solution to the problem typically involved an important reduction in total investment costs to the client because the management fee was reduced by the amount of portfolio brokerage "offset." As a result, the broker-manager's clients often had lower total costs—management fee plus brokerage charges—than the clients of other managers who paid a full fee and full brokerage charges. In brief, the apparent conflict of interest was quickly and easily resolved to the advantage of the broker-manager's clients, who paid lower total costs for investment services than were paid by clients of non-brokers.

The Committee later expanded on this point to develop in some detail the basis for their conclusion that the hidden conflicts were more serious in practice than the apparent conflicts. For example, while bank trust departments had seemed quite immune to portfolio-turnover conflicts, Senate testimony had shown that bankers had had a direct interest in their total volume of brokerage commissions and the allocation of commissions among brokers, because through demand-deposit reciprocal arrangements, the bankers had recaptured their trust-department brokerage commissions and, without client knowledge, had significantly increased their commercial banking profits. And mutual funds had used the extra profitability of high commissions to pay brokers to sell their funds. And insurance companies had, in effect, paid brokers to buy insurance from them. And investment counselors had used commissions to induce brokers to feed them new clients. And, of course, brokers had paid for meals and trips and other personal luxuries that investment managers had enjoyed but had not reported to their clients. The Committee concluded that the investment business was fraught with important conflicts between the interests of the clients and the interests of the investment community, and that brokers and managers were not antagonists, but rather allies—partners in an economic collusion that neither wished to change; that both were living well off the cost of brokerage transactions, which was for them a "soft dollar" currency in vast supply, but was, of course, ultimately real money and a real cost to the clients; and that the clients were, in a real sense, the American people: insurance-policy holders, pensioners, mutual-fund shareholders and individual investors.

The Committee members were not so naïve as to believe that reciprocity was the only problem with institutional commissions. The money managers often seemed simply not to care how much the commission costs were. After all, it didn't cost *them* anything. These costs were paid by the client. It was all Other People's Money. And the clients didn't require a careful accounting of these commission costs. So the money managers tended to be sloppy. But if the commissions were paid by the money managers, their own economic self-interest would discipline the process.

The members of the Committee agreed that significant reform of the stock market, reform that would meet their goal of cost minimization, would only be possible if this *sub rosa* system of interlocking financial ties and reciprocal arrangements could be broken. And that could only be done by taking away the powerful financial incentive to "get along by going along," to take advantage of the two tiers of client costs: management fees and brokerage commissions. Double charging must be eliminated.

While more experienced and sophisticated minds might have scoffed at its naïveté, Moss and his colleagues agreed to a simple idea: *Everybody should be a broker.* More precisely, every investment organization should offer brokerage or stock-clearing services to its customers without charge, just as they usually offered such services as certificate custody, record keeping, statement preparation, tax records and daily trading and dividend notices.

The Committee plan would not force investment managers actually to become brokers or Exchange members.

That would be a matter of individual choice. But all investment managers would be required to charge their customers a single overall investment management fee and then to provide for transaction clearance either by joining the Exchange or by subcontracting the clearing function to Exchange members *at the manager's own expense.* (Of course, firms that chose not to offer investment-management services could offer a lower-cost brokerage-only service to individual and institutional investors who wanted to have just the basic transaction clearance services.)

For the banks, mutual funds and other institutions, this would be a simple enough change in operations because they were already staffed to perform most of the functions that brokers performed anyway. By making them part of the Exchange organization, the main effect would be elimination of broker-middlemen, which would help cut costs considerably.

Some Committee members were concerned about the impact of this change on the retail brokerage firms that dealt primarily with the general public. What about Merrill Lynch? As they discussed the issues, they became convinced that Merrill Lynch was itself an institution, that it was much like the large investment-counsel firms, and that it could charge for its services an advisory fee that was based on customers' assets instead of a brokerage commission on trading turnover. (Customers who insisted on actively trading their accounts might be charged a service charge for abnormal trading volume.) The Committee was determined to see to it that individual investors who wanted only execution services would not have to pay excessive brokerage commissions and that individuals seeking investment advice would pay for that advice on the basis of the assets invested, not the frequency of changes in recommendations by the broker or investment adviser.

It was a disarmingly simple solution. The Exchange mechanism would be open to all investment managers. Free competitive forces could be counted on to assure investors valuable services at reasonable prices. And by taking away the protected profit of brokerage commissions, the conflicts between the investment industry and its customers would simply dry up. No profit, no conflicts. All members would want to keep transaction costs down because these costs were now to be paid directly by the members.

The Committee members agreed that their proposals were probably going to prove too radical for adoption by the existing New York and American Exchanges, and that it would probably be wise to think in terms of creating a new securities exchange. This idea proved to have many advantages. New management could be more easily obtained by starting over than by grafting a new group onto an old and probably inbred structure. Creating a new exchange would make it much easier to consolidate all trading in a central marketplace with a single mechanism for reporting all transactions (the so-called Big Tape). Effective regulation would be much easier to achieve. And so, one of the basic components of the Committee's overall program became the creation of the Federal Securities Exchange, which would have headquarters in Washington, D.C., and would be under the direction of an independent Board of Governors which was patterned closely on the model of the Federal Reserve Board of Governors. The seven Governors were to be appointed by the President for overlapping terms of six years. Self-regulation in the stock market had been, the Committee concluded, a failure.

The Committee then chose to take a ten-week recess to evaluate their own work. They soon concluded that they had not given adequate attention to the risk-taking function of market makers. In particular, they had ignored the vital role of dealers who would commit their own capital and risk financial loss in the hope of earning a profit by "making a market" and absorbing excess supply or providing supply when demand was temporarily high. In other words, the Committee found that they had entirely ignored the block-bidding firms, the Specialists on the floors of the exchanges, the arbitrageurs, and all the over-the-counter market makers. Without these essential market-making intermediaries and their risk capital, the traditional market mechanism would not work well.

For a time, it appeared that the Committee would have to abandon its new scheme in order to protect the historic vitality of the marketplace, but fortunately a great deal of quantitative data about the operation of the market had been collected during the SEC's Special Study of Institutional Investing, and as the Committee met in executive session with key members of the SEC's group, they concluded that arbitrage should not be affected by the proposed changes because arbitrageurs trade almost exclusively for their own accounts; that OTC trading could be made a regular part of the Federal Securities Exchange, including immediate full disclosure of trades; and that the floor-specialist function could be eliminated by automation. However, a limited number of block-positioning dealers would be essential for the efficient functioning of the FSE. The Committee decided to add dealers to their system and agreed that a select group of dealers should submit sealed competitive bids for a limited number of four-year terms as Authorized Dealers on the Federal Securities Exchange.

Authorized Dealers would not be members of the FSE as brokers. Their sole function would be as market makers —they would buy or sell positions in stocks, using their own capital, whenever normal supply and demand were out of balance on the FSE. They would be taking risks, but they would also be earning rewards by, on average, selling at higher prices than they bought in the classic dealer function. The Committee felt that having seven such dealers would provide adequate competition between dealers and yet assure them of an attractive incentive to commit their capital to what they readily agreed was a high-risk business. No other firms would be empowered to act as dealers in equity securities on the Federal Stock Exchange.

The consolidation of formerly listed stock trading and OTC trading on the FSE was made possible by an important new development in computer technology which had been tested and proven feasible as the NASD-Automatic Quotation Service, Autex and Instinet. The basic equipment involved a cathode-ray-tube display unit, a very large time-share computer in which all buying and selling interests in each stock could be stored, and a set of controls by means of which the data bank could be interrogated quickly and reliably. The several systems had worked well in the supporting role of helping brokers collect and disseminate price and volume information widely and cheaply; but it had been generally assumed that such devices could only be supportive and that ultimately men must make the final trades with men. Moss and his associates, after lengthy investigation and much thought, concluded that the principal reason people believed "men must talk to men" was because that was the way things had been done, and not because it was necessarily so. They concluded that if most, if not all, of the humans involved in the transaction process could be removed, then machines could interact with machines with important benefits in speed, reliability and cost reduction. So they set about determining how to eliminate the need for people in the Exchange system.

Ultimately, the case for having people negotiate the price of every individual trade came down to one argument. Only people could take risks with capital, and risk-taking was the essence of making continuous markets that were broad, deep and resilient. The Moss Committee took careful aim at that primary target. They were confident that the relatively small risks of mis-estimating the daily and hourly fluctuations of prices could be allocated to and absorbed by Exchange users as one of the regular costs of operations. The SEC study staff demonstrated to the Committee, using their extensive historical trading statistics, that the operating costs of the Specialist system were so large that an unsophisticated iterative computer program could be operated at a far, far lower cost than the Specialist system, even after absorbing errors and such abrupt shifts in market behavior as those triggered by the Cuban missile crisis, LBJ's resignation, and the Nixon wage- and price-freeze announcements.

The one ingredient needed to make the SEC group's program operational was active buyer and seller participation in the marketplace. The one great advantage of the Specialist system was that the Specialist was always ready to buy or sell. The problem with an automated system was that potential buyers and potential sellers might not notice that stock prices were changing and that their "price conditional" interest should be converted to active buying or selling. Widespread usage of automatic display devices would help, and so would the Big Tape, but this was probably not enough. It might take a day or more for potential buyers to become real buyers during a price slump, or for potential sellers to become actual sellers during a price run-up, and prompt response to relatively small price movements was considered essential to an orderly, continuous market.

This apparently unsolvable problem was surprisingly easy to handle. The SEC group suggested that the standard stabilization procedures used on the commodities markets could be readily adapted to the new stock market. The price of a stock would be allowed to change no more than 2 percent during a single trading session. Whenever any stock had changed by that maximum amount during a day's trading, it would stop trading for the rest of the day or until enough selling or buying interest was stimulated among Exchange members to bring the stock price back into the "plus or minus 2 percent range" and reopen trading activity. With this limit on price change in a single day, Moss was convinced the automated Federal Securities Exchange would not only achieve a better market but also would operate at a small fraction of the cost of the old broker-cum-dealer system of the New York and American Exchanges. As soon as any stock reached the 2 percent limit, it would be shown in a special display of "limited" stocks flashed regularly to all FSE market members to encourage active interest in the stock by members who might, at the new price, want to buy or sell. And with the limit on price changes, the selected Authorized Dealers who would be admitted to Exchange membership would know more about their risk of loss in making position bids and so should be more willing to take on large blocks of stock; this would also contribute to the market's liquidity because the dealers could use their capital more aggressively and take larger positions in more stocks than under the old Exchange system of unlimited risk and *caveat emptor.*

The "2 percent plus or minus price limit" later became known as the "anti-speculation" provision because it was assumed that the 2 percent rule would give all market members sufficient time to fully reappraise the value of a stock and to determine whether they wanted to buy or sell, as the case might be. If no investors wanted to act on the limit price, the price would move 2 percent each day until it reached the price at which investors wanted to become active buyers or sellers. However, while the price was changing rapidly enough to be governed by the 2 percent rule, there would be no trading. If investors were aware of the impossibility of swift escape from surprise adversities, then investors would be more cautious in their buying and would be less willing to play according to the Greater Fool Theory, the investor's version of Old Maid. Moss also believed that individual investors would be better protected from what he called "institutional red-dogging"—the aggressive dumping of a stock by professionals who learn of unfavorable company developments and quickly sell their stock to innocent individual investors who have left open orders to buy with their brokers.

The Moss Committee had completed the basic reorientation of the securities markets before the summer recess of Congress. When they reconvened in the fall of 1971, they were convinced that they had resolved the major issues before them and so directed their attention to a long series of specific items. The first of these would be defining the scope of responsibility of the new Federal Securities Exchange Board of Governors and its staff.

The Committee was anxious not to limit unnecessarily the authority of the Board of Governors, and so chose to avoid questions of policy or procedure whenever possible and to concentrate instead on identifying specific goals and objectives. They recognized that a clearly laid out "intent of Congress" could be a powerful administrative guide and judicial support to a regulatory body, particularly a new one; so their records disclosed in detail the areas rejected and the areas accepted by the Committee as the Board's responsibility.

The Committee was convinced that one of the major tasks of the Board of Governors should be an overhauling of the system of financial reporting to investors by American corporations. While unwilling to bind the Board by pointing out specific items, the Committee clearly included the development and maintenance of an effective means of fairly reporting corporate earnings.

The Committee did identify two specific proposals which it thought worthy of special consideration by the Board of Governors. The first was a requirement that all publicly owned companies file an up-to-date prospectus with the Board at least once each year, whether or not an issue of securities were contemplated. This annual prospectus was to be distributed to all shareholders as part of the traditional annual report to stockholders. This, they suggested, would increase disclosure of important information on a regular, comprehensive and systematic basis.

The second specific proposal was that managements of FSE-listed companies be forbidden from meeting privately with any special investor or investor groups about company affairs. The Committee could find no reason for any such meetings other than to obtain for one group of shareholders an advantage over other groups of shareholders, and this kind of favoritism did not seem a proper activity for management.

The Moss Committee also suggested a thirty-day advance-notice requirement before insiders could buy or sell shares in their companies, on the theory that if insiders were buying or selling for other than long-term reasons, they might be taking improper advantage of their own shareholders in the public marketplace. If the investments were truly long term in character, then the advance notice should be no problem.

The Committee proposed a large increase in the budget for stock-market supervision and suggested that a combination staff of former SEC officials and Federal bank supervisors would be appropriate, but again left the final judgments to the new Board of Governors. However, the Committee did affirm its expectation that supervisory regulations of Exchange numbers would be at least as careful and comprehensive as the supervision of the nation's commercial banks and that the financial condition of members would be made public regularly.

The Committee took direct action to eliminate the onerous stock certificate. They specifically provided the legal basis for demonstrating legally enforceable ownership rights without the physical evidence of stock-certificate possession that had been previously considered so important by attorneys, and they directed the FSE to eliminate certificates by July 1, 1973.

The Committee considered and then decided to pass on to Wilbur Mills's Ways and Means Committee four items of tax reform. The first extended the holding period for qualified long-term capital gains from the previous six months to a period of three years. The second proposal would impose a capital-gains tax on foreign investors. It was not to apply to individual stock sales, which would continue to be untaxed as long as the sale proceeds were promptly reinvested in other U.S. securities, but would apply to net withdrawals of funds from the American market. This, it was hoped, would reduce the risk of another massive outflow of capital in future bear-market periods. The third proposal was that the unrelated business income tax should be extended to include all capital gains or trading profits from pension-fund portfolio management that were not long term in nature. This proposal was aimed at curtailing the very aggressive go-go investing that had begun to gain favor among pension funds and endowment funds in the late sixties. The fourth proposal was aimed directly at the hedge funds and would prohibit capital-gains treatment of compensation of investment managers. Such treatment had been allowed previously when fund managers were made participating partners along with their investor clients. Representative Mills indicated genuine interest in the specific propositions and a serious concern for the principals involved and promised to take them up in his Committee.

The Moss Committee urged the new Board of Governors to consider applying the basic concept of the Prudent Man Rule to all FSE members and laid particular stress on the importance of mutual-fund directors and pension-fund trustees maintaining genuine independence in their decisions.

The Committee made two major decisions about the business activities of FSE members. First, it adopted the Canadian approach and specifically recommended the separation of trust departments from commercial banks, arguing that this move was only an updating of the Glass-Steagall Act's separation of lender and equity investor that had originally split off the investment bankers from the commercial bankers. To balance this proposal, the Committee suggested a careful reconsideration by the Board of Governors of the prohibition against trust departments offering mutual funds and other financial services to the public. Moss and his colleagues were strongly persuaded that, in fact, banks should be encouraged to offer mutual funds, particularly no-load funds, as an efficient means of providing professional management to small investors.

If trust departments were separated from commercial banks, the Committee felt they should be encouraged to provide a wide range of financial services to individuals, including insurance and brokerage.

The other separation was a unanimously approved separation of underwriting from brokerage. The Committee was convinced that the paramount importance of "strong distribution" in the underwriting business had led to a clear conflict of interest in which brokers were heavily rewarded for "distributing the merchandise" without proper regard for the suitability of the securities to the investors' needs and objectives. As a result, many serious conflicts of interest and unsavory practices had come to characterize underwriting. The means of implementing this major reform was simple: no underwriter could be a Broker Member (but could be an Authorized Dealer) on the Federal Securities Exchange. This would force an arms-length negotiation on price of security offerings between the expert representative of the seller (the underwriter) and the expert representatives of the buyers (the FSE members).

Taken all together, the legislation which the Moss Committee so carefully researched and so painstakingly drafted was clearly the most comprehensive and far reaching reform legislation in forty years. Among professional investors, the enormity of the achievement was epitomized by the hypothetical FSE user charges that had been worked out by the Committee staff using actual trading volume and estimated FSE transaction costs. For Prudential Insurance the average monthly fee was $12,500. For the Dreyfus Fund it was $187,432. For IDS the fee was less than $80,000. For Morgan Guaranty it was $80,500. And for institutional investors and their clients all over the nation, the user charges worked out to approximately 10 percent of what the total costs of brokerage commissions had been. The Committee estimated annual operating costs of the entire Federal Securities Exchange at less than $500 million compared to the former costs of more than $5 billion.

The reaction to the report of the Moss Committee which was made public in early July of 1972 was "mixed." Wall Streeters were outraged, overwhelmed, incredulous and angry. The public reaction was so positive, in contrast, that Moss, to his own obvious surprise, had attained the national prominence which so many of his colleagues in the Senate had been so actively seeking. Moss modestly explained, "We have laid the basis for an institutional securities system for a very simple reason: The market is dominated by institutions, it already is their market on a *de facto* basis, and we simply recognized the realities of the situation and made it *de jure*. The market was reorganized under Congressional action in the early thirties to provide a sound and equitable system for individual investors. Now, forty years later, we have simply recognized the primary role of the institutional investor and have provided a sound and equitable system to meet the needs of institutional investors who manage funds for the American people.

"We have also helped the individual investor get a

better deal and a fair deal by safeguarding his interests from abuse—whether intended or not—from the operations of institutions and the temptations of brokers to churn his account and to stick him with low-quality underwritings."

Chapter 7 THE CORPORATE EXECUTIVE

MANY PEOPLE in Congress, in Wall Street and across the land felt that the work of the Moss Committee had provided a fair and final solution to the abuses of the securities industry, but an unusual conversation I had had early in 1971 with the chief executive of a major conglomerate kept coming back to me and made me feel that while Moss had changed the rules of the game, perhaps it would be impossible to legislate control over the industry unless and until somehow the players themselves were changed. And what had been done that might really change the way the people in the business behaved? I would not have been worried about all this except for the haunting memory of that conversation.

It was, I suppose, a unique opportunity. At least it was an unusual chance to see that mad sequence of events from another man's perspective while the rush of events still seemed fresh and real to us both. For most people who are on the fringes of history, it is not possible to get the unedited, unrehearsed, unhomogenized, still confusing story of events as seen by participants. The simple, clear stories of things past are easier to accept, easier to remember and much easier to tell. But reality is not so simple as truth. And this was not an evening of truth, but only of reality—reality as he could see it during a few brief conversational hours at my home in Connecticut. It was a private conversation which I probably would not now reveal except for its importance in understanding the 1971 Crash.

"Do you have any regrets?" I asked.

"No, not really. If you had asked me just a few days ago, I'd have said something like 'Yeah. I wish it had never ended,' but that's really bullshit. It was a game, a great game. Maybe the greatest game ever. And I played the whole game for all it was worth—for all I was worth, anyway, and for all I could get out of it while it lasted. But every game has to be over sometime. If it could go on forever, it wouldn't really be a game, would it? If it could last, it wouldn't be as much fun to play. Any really good game has to have an ending and the ending has to be beyond the control of the players. That's the only essential rule of the game: It will stop. And you or anybody else might get caught and then, bang-bang, you lose. You lose it all. Regrets? Yeah, one. I only wish I hadn't been caught quite so hard."

There was a pause as he stared at the fire and then stirred the lemon twist in his glass with his finger. "But maybe that's bullshit too. I didn't play to win. Only to be winning. If I had to run a real company, I'd get bored in no time. I like deals. Doing deals is my specialty. Lots of guys can run companies but damned few can put 'em together. Damned few guys can do good deals. And even fewer can do deals fast and creative.

"Sure, I'm off the field now. On the sidelines. But nobody did deals better than me. Nobody."

"What deal was your favorite? Not American?"

"No, that was pretty straightforward. By then we had quite a road show. We could field accountants and lawyers and investment bankers in platoons. American was big, sure, the biggest take-over ever done; but it was kind of dull, really. By the time we did American, we had our operation down so pat it was kind of conventional. Besides, American was too big for real creativity. And it was mostly done by outsiders: accountants, lawyers, proxy solicitors, bankers and brokers. All we had to do was say "Go" and they cranked it out for us. I never thought of American as our deal or my deal. That was their deal. I don't even think we would have gone along except we had to have something big, we had to be making news or we were going to be in trouble, bad trouble. And as any Marine knows, the only defense when they close in on you is to move out—fast. It doesn't much matter which way you run."

"But you got clobbered doing American. At least that was the last deal you did before the company landed in bankruptcy court."

"Don't remind me. But at least we went down in style. Besides, we might have made it if those bastards in the Street hadn't screwed everything all up. What the hell do you suppose is gonna happen to us when we're doing the high wire act and those clowns pull the whole damned tent down on everybody?

"What a bunch of jerks those guys are. The only thing

that counts in Wall Street is money. Money, money, money, money. There's no reality in that business—everything is for sale. And for sale all day long. Maybe you can't really blame them for losing touch. I mean if you think you can buy and sell General Motors any time of any day—and that's exactly what they think they're doing when they trade a few blocks of GM stock—maybe you learn to have a case of megalomania. Maybe you just can't help it. Or maybe you have to con yourself so you can live with the fact that you're getting rich doing damned near nothing. Does anybody really believe that trading stocks back and forth really matters all that much?

"Every time I go to Vegas I think of Wall Street. They're almost exactly the same. Think about it. Big money is on the line all the time. The action is continuous. The little guy comes for thrills which the fat cats provide him because they need to finance their overhead. But the real action happens out in the back rooms where it's quiet and everybody plays table stakes. Out front in the casino they've got croupiers and dealers who are just like brokers in a classy boardroom. The noise is even the same—the slots sound just like the automated quote boards and there's that constant hum of people parting with their money. The words are so much alike you have to look carefully to be sure you know where you are—"double up," "let winners run," "you're covered," "I'm short," "I'm hot," and all that. But in both places the only way to really understand what's going on and why is by getting to know the principals. Both groups are interesting. Both groups are good at the same thing. They're good killers.

"But you know what's really the key? They're all for sale. Shit, you don't even have to buy the bastards. You can rent 'em. I know because I did. The only difference between the Strip and the Street is their price. On the Strip they hit you for twenty percent of the action. On the Street, it's only five percent. But then, when you buy a guy in Vegas he works strictly for you. On the Street, they got maybe a dozen other johns on the line. No wonder people think they're whores. Who knows, maybe that's why both brokers and broads live up on Park Avenue together."

"Did you form any real friendships in Wall Street?" I asked.

"Christ, no. There's no time for that. Time really is money for them and they only spoon one out when they're spooning the other back in. Besides, they aren't friend-forming people."

After fixing us two more martinis, I came back to the fireplace and asked, "How did you get started in all this?"

"Oh I don't know. I guess I always wanted to make it big. Really big. Typical stuff like coming to Manhattan with my high-school class and getting all excited about the big buildings and the limousines and all the way back to our little town in Arkansas I sat on that bus promising myself I'd be back in New York in style someday.

"A buddy and I started a construction company during college and hocked ourselves to the gills. We planned to put up a small set of garden apartments during the summer between years, but we got delayed because of heavy rains and a strike and so I had to drop out of school to keep the bank happy.

"Anyway, that operation finally worked out pretty good. We mortgaged out all the costs, got our money back right away and owned a nice rental property with a good depreciation tax shelter and a real good cash flow. We were making ten percent on our money with no money up, and I said to myself, 'Jack, old boy, this is your ticket back to Broadway.'

"So I went after real estate development in a big way. That was back in the very early sixties and it was a terrific business because gross returns were fourteen percent, maybe fifteen percent and you could get full financing for six and a half to seven percent so you could keep damned near all the spread. And the depreciation meant we never had any taxable income. One thing I am proud of: I never paid any taxes to support the Vietnam war!

"At any rate, we standardized our product line, which cut costs and also reduced our risk of poor market acceptance, and we used specially trained crews to put the projects together for us. And you know as well as I do that with no taxes and high-leverage bank financing, we could really grow. All we had to do was dream up the project locations and crank them out.

"Frankly, I thought we had a real good business. Where else can you start with nothing and make a couple of million bucks in a few years? But it really stuck in my craw that when I went to New York or Chicago or San Francisco, nobody had any idea who the hell I was. Nobody knew the company. Nobody knew me. I was making money, but I wasn't making it big. And that's really what got me in the right mood.

"Then one day a guy comes into my office and says, 'Hey! How would you like to go public?' Well, I couldn't believe it. I just sat there dumbfounded."

"You mean you couldn't believe he would ask you?"

"No. For Christ's sake, no. That isn't what surprised me. What really got to me was that I hadn't thought of it myself. I just sat there thinking what a fool I was being, what a complete and utter fool! Here we were, growing like a cancer in the housing business, which was one of Wall

Street's favorites, and we were working just for money. Of *course* we should go public. Then we'd really be on the map. And in the big time. I could hardly wait."

"And was your caller from Weber and Company?"

"No, he wasn't. He was from a small regional brokerage firm in our area. A nice enough guy, but not a real mover and doer. He was not the guy for me, even if it was his idea in a way. Ever since playing football in high school in Arkansas, I don't ever want anybody on my team who doesn't play for keeps. When I call those guys in Wall Street a bunch of killers, that's exactly what I wanted to have working for me."

"How did you get involved with Weber and Company?"

"I picked 'em because they could do the job and because they needed me."

"How did you know?"

"Oh, that wasn't too hard. First I decided that no matter what firm I went to, the whole relationship would depend on the one guy who was working with me. We'd be his client, not the firm's client. Then I figured that the ideal guy would be in an old-line firm that had a lot of prestige, but was a little thin on new ideas and new companies to bring to market because the whole underwriting business depends on just two things—new-issue originations and distribution, usually through grandfather rights to a major-bracket position in underwriting syndicates. I figured that if I could find a hungry young partner in an old-line major-bracket firm, I might be just what he was looking for to move up to a senior partnership by injecting some 'new issues' life into his sleepy firm."

"And Bill Roth at Weber was your man?"

"Yes. Actually, I found several good candidates, but Roth had a special lust to make money and I figured his greed would be insatiable and that he'd work harder and longer than the others. And he looked like the kind of guy who could deliver his own firm on anything, so I went with him and his firm."

"Do you think you made a mistake?"

"Not in my analysis. I was right about both Roth and Weber. But it didn't come clear to me for several years that Roth's coldness and jugular instincts would not only be one of our greatest strengths, but also one of our greatest weaknesses. He was much more dangerous than I had believed at the time. Of course, that was particularly true because I was willing to gamble on big plays. In retrospect, we were much too much alike. We were not good for each other for the long pull. I should have gotten onto a slower, more gentle horse. But what the hell, I'm not that kind of guy. Besides, we came out of the slot awfully fast, and maybe that running start is what made it possible to go as far and as fast as we did. And as I said before, I have no regrets. Sure I'd like to change the ending, but frankly I'd do the same things all over again if I had another chance."

"What did Roth do for you?" I asked.

"It seemed like everything. He took our little company by the hand the way a Hollywood producer takes a nubile young starlet and transforms her. He drew up a list of what were really only cosmetic changes but gave us at least some of that surface classiness that helps Wall Street market a company. It's the same thing in Wall Street or politics or P & G. It's all packaging. First, we changed the company name to United International Systems. As Bill Roth said, 'Who would ever think of Klaussen Industries as an exciting company?' "

"UIS doesn't really mean anything, does it?"

"No, it doesn't, but that was the point. We wanted a name that suggested big things but also one that was broad enough or general enough so we could go into any business we wanted. With a name like UIS, we could do almost anything we wanted."

"What other changes did you make?"

"There were really quite a few. Most of them were just decorations but they looked good. We spent a lot of dough putting out a really impressive Annual Report with buzz-words like 'synergy,' 'systems management,' 'Harvard Business School,' 'venture,' 'entrepreneurship,' 'performance,' and 'creative productivity.'

"We got new offices in the GM Building on Fifth Avenue and new auditors and lawyers and transfer agents so we could put a lot of big-time names on the company reports. It's really amazing how easy it is to get the Establishment to let you use their names if you are willing to pay a little dough. Not big dough either. The same thing with the Board of Directors. Hell, we offered to pay one thousand bucks a meeting four times a year, and look what we got: a retired Navy admiral, a Princeton economics professor, a Stanford Business School professor, a former U.S. Senator and a group of 'name' businessmen. Pretty good for a small hick company."

"Was it an active board?"

"If you mean 'Did they run the company?' you must be kidding. They never really had any idea what we were doing. As long as it looked good, they were happy as clams to come to meetings every three months with all expenses paid and pick up their dough."

"But what about later on when cracks began to appear in the wall?"

"I don't know for sure, but I really think they wanted even more not to know what we were doing. They took the party line we gave them and asked no real tough questions. After all, we started the meetings at ten A.M.

and broke for drinks and lunch at twelve so they didn't get much of a chance at us. And they never much wanted to discuss business at lunch. As long as things seemed OK, they left us alone. And by the time we got into such bad trouble that even they knew about it, it was too late."

"How long was it from the time you and Roth first met until UIS had its first public offering?"

"That took almost six months. We used the time to do all the cosmetic things we've just been talking about, but the main delay was in reorganizing our financial statements and getting the new financials approved by the SEC."

"What was involved in redoing your financial statements?"

"Quite a lot, really. Remember I said we had to pay no taxes? That also meant we had no reported earnings. We had paid no taxes because we earned no money—at least according to the financial records we had been using before we went public.

"You see, we had been growing pretty fast in terms of the number of buildings we put up or the number of people we had working for us or the value of the projects we were doing. But it didn't show up in profits because we were taking accelerated depreciation to be damned sure we didn't get any reported—and taxable—earnings. So we sat down with the accountants, decided how much profit we wanted to show, adopted the accounting policies that would give us the result we wanted, and then re-worked the numbers to get it. Basically a lot of this could be done just by using less of a depreciation charge, but we wanted to show even faster growth in per share earnings, so we decided to book some of the projects as though they had been sold after they had been depreciated. These two changes made enough difference to convert us from Klaussen Industries with no profits and no growth to United International Systems with $5 million in profits and a per share earnings growth rate of thirty percent a year for five straight years. That sort of thing looks awfully good on a prospectus. You know, even I was impressed."

"Your stock came out in early 1967 at thirty-five dollars and then rose to seventy-five by year end. What was behind that rapid appreciation?"

"Lots and lots of things. First, we reported just over a dollar a share earnings for '66 and then made almost two bucks in '67 so our growth rate was up and analysts were looking for maybe three dollars or three fifty in '68. And of course, we were already making some pretty good acquisitions, so it was always possible that we would hit it bigger than the analysts expected of us. But I think the best thing going for us was the small float on our stock. With relatively few shares outstanding, Weber and Company could pretty well control the price by bringing in more and more of their individual discretionary accounts and some of the more aggressive institutional buyers like the hedge funds who would buy anything so long as they were promised that the other funds would be buying in with them to keep the price going up."

"That sounds like an old-fashioned stock market pooling operation."

"Well, in a sense, it was a pool, but not with the formality and discipline of the old pools. This was more of an understanding than an agreement. And you can bet there were no records kept and no contracts and no letters. A thin stock is pretty easy to run up with a few thousand shares of aggressive buying. Our stock acted, as they say, 'very well.'

"Most of the people who decide to sell their company

get there by deciding first that their company is in trouble. They hate to admit their own incompetence or failure, so they really want to make a deal with a winner because it looks like they are trading up instead of giving up. And of course we did a lot to be sure that we had that winner's image. As I said before, we spent a lot of dough in stockholder reports and then sent them to everybody even remotely connected with Wall Street and money. And we spent a bundle on that PR firm to get stories in *Business Week* and *Time* and in the papers. I guess we were pretty good copy because we got an awful lot of mileage out of the media. I even went on the Johnny Carson show once. Looking back on it, I think we got a bigger bang for the buck from the money we spent on PR than any other way. And we tried 'em all, let me tell you. We tried 'em all."

"How many acquisitions did you make during 1967?"

"Fourteen. We could have made two more, but decided they were too obviously situations involving management bail-out so we let them go."

"When you are making that many acquisitions, how can you be sure you know what you're getting?"

"Oh, you can't possibly know for sure what you are buying. I always assume the other guy is trying to bag me, and that he's got not one but two or even three enormous problems in his company. And I also figure we'll miss one or two of the toughest problems when we go in. So the first thing we do is get him to sign what we call 'The Letter.' That's our secret weapon and it is worth a fortune. It looks like a standard letter of intent but it is really a hunting license for us to go into the company's books and records for a full ninety days and learn everything about the way they run their business. The best part is that when they sign the letter, they are fully committed. They can't get away from us if we decide later that we want them. But for us, there are so many hidden ways we can get off the hook that it's really no commitment at all. And this is a very big help when we come to the end of our three-month option period and it's time to fix the price on the deal. By then, we've really done a job on them and we can screw the final price down nice and tight. And this way, we wind up paying a lot less than it looks to be worth so we can absorb one or two bad surprises later on."

"Don't they ever complain?"

"Of course they do. They all kick and holler. But they're stuck. You see, they've already decided to sell out. Then they let us go all over their operations and learn all their secrets. They are scared stiff we'll call it off and then play 'kiss and tell.' They need us more than we need them, really. We know what we're doing when we get into these negotiations, but for them it's usually the first time.

"Then during the last few days of negotiations, while the tension is really getting to them, we take each of the key people off to one side and design a package deal for them individually. Sometimes it is titles and stuff like that. Some guys want an executive jet. Others want a limo and driver. And of course, they all want a fat raise. So we take maybe half a million bucks and lay it on them the right way and wind up saving maybe fifty or a hundred million dollars on the purchase price. In other words, we give them $500,000 and save maybe ten times that in interest charges at the bank, so it's a good deal for them and a good deal for us."

"But not for their stockholders?"

"You can't always say that. For one thing, we always offer more than the going market for their stock and they're usually greedy enough to want it. And for another thing, so what? What's so sacred about stockholders? I don't buy all this crap about everybody working for the little old stockholder. They're just as greedy as anybody else."

"You've had a lot of experience with institutional investors. What are your thoughts on how they operate?" I asked.

"That all depends. I got to know a lot of different people from the institutions: analysts, brokers, fund managers, hedge-fund operators, bankers, insurance people, traders. Old guys and young guys. Some very smart cookies and some real dumbbells. I can't generalize except for one thing: Much as they like to talk about quality of management, the long term and value judgment, I never met one guy who wasn't mostly interested in price. They really mean it when they say buy low and sell high. They haven't any kind of an interest in really staying with a company. They want to get in and get out as fast as they can make a buck doing it. Of course, they think that being sharp on price is their strong suit. Maybe it is. But if that's their big strength, it is also for damned sure their big weakness because they are so consumed by prices that they can be had easy."

"What do you mean?"

"Well, let's take an example. I want to do a deal. I want to do it nice 'n' easy. No problem. All I got to do is go to one institutional broker and tell him I want to meet him up at my suite at the Regency. He comes by about six and I swear him to secrecy and offer him a chance to do half a million shares of stock and he says 'Sure. How?' and I lay out the terms I'm willing to offer on a take-over bid and give him a set of pro forma earnings projections, assuming the deal gets done. All I ask him to do is arrange meetings with a few institutions that understand the

advantages of cooperation and mutually beneficial interests. Then we go see these fund managers and tell them
what we have in mind, and explain to them in very simple
language how they can make big bucks just by going
along with us. All they got to do is warehouse a few
hundred thousand shares for a few months and we'll buy
up all they got maybe twenty-thirty percent above what
they pay. They make damned good money for their investors and show good performance. And we get a sure
deal. Everybody's happy. It's synergy, as they say in the
Street."

"You make synergy sound like a social disease."

"Maybe it is. One thing's sure, if they think they can
make money at it, it doesn't matter what it is, they'll do
it. It's unbelievable. The institutional guys really believe
in the fast buck. Matter of fact, that's really all they
believe in."

"Did you have other contact with the institutions?"

"Oh, we were in virtually constant contact. Every day
or so another analyst would come in to see us."

"How did you deal with them?"

"I tried to see them all myself because we had concepts
that we wanted to get across. First it was 'residential
development,' then 'shelter systems,' then as we got
further away from housing, it became 'fiscal productivity
in leisure time' and things like that."

"But why did you spend so much time with analysts
instead of on the operations of your business?"

"Isn't that pretty obvious? Our stock always came first.
We had to keep our price-earnings ratio up. I mean if the
analysts didn't believe in our ability to produce earnings
and gains in per share earnings, our stock multiple would
go down. We needed that P/E to do good deals, and as
long as we had the P/E, we could do lots of good deals

and deliver on the earnings the institutions wanted. It worked all the way around. They were happy, we were happy."

"You make it sound easy. Was it?"

"Yes and no. I mean we couldn't hand them just any old line of bull. It had to be plausible enough for them to swallow. But frankly, when you're doing a lot of deals, it's not too hard to make out a case that you're really a growth company."

"Why is that?"

"First of all, they really want to believe you. Like I say, they're greedy, and if you show them an easy way to make money, they'll try hard to see it your way. Second, you hold all the cards in terms of accounting, and the accountants will go along with almost anything because they're scared of losing the business you give them. So you look down the list of things you can do to change earnings. You can cut out research. Depreciation can be slowed down. Marketing costs can be cut. Increase the actuarial rate of return assumption on the pension fund. Sell off some land or depreciated plant and lease it back and you can flow the capital gain into earnings. Or sell out the stocks of take-over candidates that rushed into a marriage with some other company—also at a capital gain. Most old-line companies are pretty conservative in their accounting so there's usually a lot we can do whenever we want to boost earnings. Most of the time you don't even need these kinds of things because if you buy a low-multiple company with high P/E paper you automatically create 'earnings' gains."

"You mean because if you have a twenty-P/E stock and use it to buy ten-P/E stocks, you automatically increase your earnings per share."

"Right. It's like I told the analysts. 'You give me the

P/E and I'll give you the EPS.' Of course, they don't really care how I get the earnings so long as they come through, and I made it my business to deliver up earnings every quarter."

"Did you find any one group of institutions harder than the others to deal with? Was any one group really different from the others?"

"No, I don't think so. I mean everybody assumed the hedge funds were an easy mark, and they were. But so was everybody else."

"Can you be more specific?"

"Sure. We went to banks, particularly banks that had been the prime banks for companies we acquired and we laid it on the line: 'You believe in us and we'll believe in you. You buy our stock for your pension accounts and we'll use you as a lender.' It's the old 'You scratch my back and I'll scratch yours.' They all went along. Some acted like they didn't like it, but they all went along.

"Brokers were the same. For example, say we decide to buy five hundred thousand shares of stock before making a merger offer. We take six or ten months and do the whole thing very quiet. This means we have just one broker acquiring the stock. For a broker, that's easy, easy business. All he's got to do is keep his mouth shut and he gets thirty cents a share, which is one hundred and fifty grand. All we ask is they write us up in their research department and recommend our stock to their clients. They help us, we help them.

"The investment bankers are even easier. They all jawbone about how cautious they are about putting their name on a prospectus, but let me tell you from firsthand experience, when I offer some guy half a million bucks in fees or discounts, I'm here to tell you I can get any house in Wall Street to stand up and salute. I mean any house.

Any one at all. At any time. It may sound unbelievable, but it's sure true. I know. Because I've had some of the best."

"What about the arbitrageurs?"

"Those cats? They're terrific. I mean they are so very predictable. All you have to do is show them a merger where they can make a fat profit, and then keep feeding them current information about how the deal is going, and they'll go all the way with you. In many ways, they're better partners than the institutions. Partly because they don't have anybody looking over their shoulder. Partly they can take a thinner gross profit. Partly they can take short-term profits. And partly they are more willing to try a crap shoot. And, of course, they go in with big dollars when they go, so it's a little bit like having Sam Huff blocking for you. They are bastards, you know, but they're my kind of bastards. You always know exactly where they stand. Near the money. Very, very near the money."

"What about the institutional research analysts? Are they as big a deal as we're led to believe?"

"Yes and no. Honestly, I didn't think most of them were all that hot. They talk about careful financial analysis and field work checking out our customers, our suppliers, our competitors and all that. But that's just talk. At least in my own experience it was just talk. They never really did their homework. None of them really knew what was going on in the company. And they didn't really seem to care.

"You hear a lot of stuff about investing in really well-managed companies, but as far as Wall Street is concerned, the only thing that really counts is whether your stock is going up or going down. If the stock has been going up, you're well managed. If the stock has been going up a lot, you are a creative management destined to achieve great things. If the stock has been going down, all your executives are clowns and you have no ability at all to run a company. Look at duPont: in the fifties they were God's gift to American corporate management and then in the sixties they dropped way down. Why? Same people and the same management concepts, so it can't really be due to management deterioration. Their problem was simple—the chemical industry went from being one of the best industries to one of the worst. It was as simple as that. But Wall Street people persist in believing their own myths that it isn't the external opportunity but the internal management that makes for good profits and strong stocks. You'd think they'd realize that the only really good way to make really good earnings is to be in the right place at the right time. And that ain't management, brother, that is luck. Mind you, I've got nothing against good luck; I just don't see why Wall Street isn't willing to see it for what it is.

"The other thing about the crowd from the Street is that they are always talking to each other. I mean if I tell one or two analysts something, it only takes two or three days for anybody who gives a damn to have all that I said reported to him by at least a dozen 'independent' sources. Whispering to one broker's analyst is like standing on a table and shouting out the news at Locke-Ober's or Oscar's.

"The other aspect of this fantastic thing they've got for getting the word around is that they all want to teach you how to behave, how to take advantage of their own system. Once they buy your stock, they want you to look good to everybody else. They coach you and coach you on how to do a snow job on Wall Street. They give you tips on what to say, what not to say, when to say it, who to say it to. Everything. It's amazing. Like they have a secret game and will take you by the hand and teach you all the secrets so you can win their secret game. You can't help but look good by the time they finish shaping you up."

"Why do they do that?"

"Simple. At least I think it's simple. They don't really care about the truth. All they want is a stock that doubles. So as soon as one guy buys your stock, he starts teaching you what to say and do, so everybody else will buy your stock and run it up."

"But no stock can go up forever on just a lot of smooth talking. Or can it?"

"No, of course it can't. But each individual analyst or broker or fund manager assumes he will be the first to get out, or at least one of the first to sell out, so he's glad to do anything to get the stock up as high as possible before he decides to sell."

"And you go along because it helps you do more acquisitions."

"Right. The higher our P/E, the easier it was for us to do good deals. And the more deals we did, the better our earnings. For us, it was great. We had all of Wall Street and all the institutions on our side. They were all working for us—bringing us deals, pressing fund managers to buy our stock, dreaming up 'concepts' to articulate our business strategy, showing us how to manage our earnings, giving us advice on what to put in our stockholder reports and even showing us how to structure deals. I don't know how you would measure it, but at one time or another we had somewhere between fifty and five hundred experts from Wall Street telling us how to win their game. It's like having all the big wheels in Las Vegas telling you exactly how to break the bank at the casino. You're damned right I went along. All the way. I learned every trick they had to offer, and used them all."

"What were some of the tricks of the trade?"

"Boy, that could take all night."

"Well, pick out just a few of the techniques you used to get the earnings up."

"O.K. Take the typical old-line industrial company. They've got a pension fund for their employees. Lots of times the contribution to the pension fund each year is as big as pretax earnings. Now that's a big item. We did two things in a situation like that. First, a man usually wasn't entitled automatically to any benefits unless he worked to age sixty-five and retirement. So when we'd take over, we'd talk up a big drive to cut costs, and the easiest way to cut costs was to fire people and cut back the payroll. Well, we'd make sure to get rid of the guys who were getting close to retirement for two reasons. First, you can usually hire a twenty-five-year-old Harvard MBA for about half what most people pay a sixty-year-old school-of-hard-knocks alumnus who has come up through the ranks and is a nice guy but slow and not too bright. The MBA can and will run circles around him. The second thing is that you get a tremendous break on the pension costs by laying off the people who are about to start collecting, and in that way reducing your past-service obligation by getting rid of the guys you are obligated to. This sort of thing can cut your true employment costs—salaries plus fringe—by at least a third for the whole company.

"The other thing we did on the pension fund was to jack up the actuarial assumption. Every pension fund plan has a basic assumption about the rate of return that will be earned in future years on the money the company has contributed to the pension fund. In a lot of older companies, the rate of return assumption is only three percent or three-and-a-half percent. Now, a typical take-over candidate might be paying two million bucks into the pension fund. We come along and say 'That's ridiculous. We can run money better than that. We can earn six percent or eight percent on the money already invested in the pension fund.' And then we turn to the consulting actuary and say to him, 'Hey, what happens to the amount of money you say we have to put into that little old pension fund if we switch from a three percent assumption to a seven percent assumption?' and he says, 'Well, gee, according to my slide rule that would make such a tremendous difference that you could skip making new money contributions for two years or more,' and we say 'Golly, cousins, ain't that great? Well, that's what we'll just have to do,' and we drop the pension contribution to zero and double the reported earnings of that acquisition right away. Or maybe we raise the rate of return assumption gradually over three years and show thirty-five percent compound growth in the acquisition's earnings. Of course, when it comes to Annual Report time, we talk about synergy, entrepreneurial management, productivity, asset redeployment and all that stuff. And we might run out a separate analysis of the growth of acquired companies' earnings to con the public into thinking we were great corporate development managers. Actually all we were doing was repackaging the same old dogs, but if investors wanted to believe in fairy stories, we were willing to supply them with some pretty good screen plays. I still think it's impressive what can be done if you control the way profits are reported. You don't have to be any good at all as a line executive if you are able to control the way a company's earnings are reported. It's like playing a very complicated card game and being able to change the rules and the way the score is kept whenever and however you want to. You're certain to win one way or another, because you virtually decide what winning means. I like that kind of game."

"You've been talking about income statement changes. What were you able to do to the balance sheet?"

"There are a lot of other rinky-dinks we used to do on the P and L, but if you want to swing over to the balance sheet, there's a whole batch of things we did there.

"The most important thing was to use as much debt leverage as possible. For example, we'd buy Company A with an exchange of stock so they could sell out on a tax-free exchange. Then we'd take their balance sheet over to the bank and hock it for enough cash to make a fast tender offer for XYZ. And then as we started buying in the XYZ stock, we'd take that back to the bank and borrow more bucks to keep buying in XYZ stock and by the time we are finished, we've bought two companies for the cash price of one. You've got to admit that for all they look tough and talk tough, the banks are willing to lend anything to anybody who is willing to pay two points over prime.

"The key thing is that if we've got a twenty P/E and we buy another company that sells at a ten P/E, we're basically buying it at half price—fifty cents on the dollar. And then we can usually turn around and borrow *our* fifty cents back from the banks and come out owning the whole show with nothing down and forever to pay. Now that's my kind of deal. Any time. All the time. I love to run the banks."

"What else?"

"Oh, I think a lot of the things we did were pretty standard stuff. Interdivisional sales agreements like the one where we set up a tiny computer company and had each division sign contracts to do all their computer work through this in-house unit. The cute part was that we scheduled each one of the contracts so this little computer company is growing at forty percent a year and has nothing but long-term sweetheart contracts. Then we take the thing public by selling twenty percent to the public and this does two things: it gives us $15 million bucks cash on the offering and a marketable security on our asset side of the balance sheet worth $60 million. And the two together mean I can go to the banks and walk out with $30-$40 million that they wouldn't otherwise let me touch. That's kind of great because all it cost us to create these assets was some legal and accounting fees and a little classic imagination. We created $75 million of new assets for less than $75,000 in legal and accounting expenses. All in less than six months. That's some return, brother. That is some rate of return. You don't see that sort of action at U.S. Steel, let me tell you."

"You did some other things with subsidiary accounting, didn't you?"

"Oh yes, we did a lot of different things. One that I liked a lot was when we saw big trouble coming in our airline sub's profits, we just hid them in the closet until the trouble was over. What we did was simple enough, but before that time nobody else had thought it up."

"How did that work exactly?" I pressed.

"Easy as pie. First, we had to get rid of about thirty percent of the stock so we could claim it was not really a subsidiary company because we only owned seventy percent of the stock and then argue that its operating earnings shouldn't be counted in our consolidated corporate earnings. What we really meant was we didn't want to have to include the losses we could see coming in a few months. So we sold a big chunk of stock to a group of institutions, cut our present ownership below required consolidation levels, deconsolidated the sub's earnings, avoided their bad earnings and kept our own stock up in the process. Then we had the sub issue new stock to buy one of our other subsidiaries, and since this move restored our percentage ownership in the airline to eighty percent, we were back in consolidation together just in time for some very good earnings in the airline business.

"Heads we win; tails we don't play. The reason the earnings were so good was that when we saw losses were inevitable, we wrote off everything. I mean *everything*. We marked down all the equipment so future depreciation would be a lot lower after we reconsolidated. We over-accrued the pension fund. Hell, we even set up a $20 million 'reserve for future contingencies,' which means if we ever need some extra profits down the road, all we have to do is dip into the honey pot and declare profits by simply revising our 'future contingency' needs.

"We even got involved with silver straddles, which are nothing but a commodity play in an effort to cut taxes. But that's too damned complicated to try and explain this late at night."

"What was it that really caught you?" I asked, sensing that the conversation was coming to an end and fearing that some of the most important topics might be passed over. "Anybody who reads your annual report for 1967 or 1968 would think you were in very solid shape. Earnings were going up fast. You were expanding rapidly. And you had an awful lot on the balance sheet. Was it the franchising or the percent-of-completion accounting that finally did you in?"

"Both, I guess. And terrible operating management. See, I know how to run a tight ship, but I really get bored on operations. I'm a deals man. So I leave the operations to other guys. But they couldn't keep up with me. I guess I had it coming. I should have known those clowns couldn't keep up with me. Wasn't it all too obvious, really? After all, I had conned each and every one of them into selling out to me on my own terms. So what should I expect? I knew they weren't really sharp. Of course they got into trouble. The problem was that my boys in the corporate control division were hard-liners and were really pressuring the operating guys to get the earnings up and to keep 'em up. So the guys on the firing line were covering up all their troubles. Some guys were even sending in phony numbers to look good. And I was too busy to notice. I was too damned cocksure, if you really want to know the truth. So when the trouble hit—Wow! Everything fell apart at once. And by then our accounting had been so badly bent out of shape that it was useless as far as finding out what was really going on. And then the accountants started changing the rules on us, and the whole thing started backing up.

"First of all, we used percent-of-completion accounting. That means when we build an apartment project, we book revenues and profits as we build the buildings. When the building is half done, we have 'earned' half the profits and half the sales price. Sounds OK, but here's the hooker: We haven't sold the building. We've got no buyer. No contract. No guarantees. No nothing. If nobody buys, we get hurt. It can be very bad. So we decide there's a great way to overcome that problem. We'll buy from ourselves. So we form a real estate investment company to buy the projects. We've got ourselves a guaranteed buyer. For anything and everything.

"We gave the public 'a chance to get in on the ground floor' and nobody understood anything about what we were doing and we raised $25 million, which we turned around and leveraged with long-term debt and bank debt so we wound up with over $100 million to buy our projects from ourselves. Since we could get ninety to ninety-five percent mortgage financing, we were now in business to build and sell more than a billion bucks worth of housing, and the buyer has got to take every project because the buyer is us. Eventually, this part of the deal got into trouble because the rental occupancy wasn't high enough to service the mortgages and the banks started calling in their loans. It was a pretty messy situation, which was really aggravated by the very tight money situation in the spring and summer of 1970. So this guaranteed buyer we've got is great except for one little thing: no mortgage money. No money means no sales. It was just like a fleet of tanks running out of gas. We were building all over the place trying to keep those damned earnings going up and all of a sudden we've got to stop. It was like the blackout. The money was flowing away from us, and in the construction business everything depends on the money flowing *to* you. You've got to have a lot of money going your way. And all of ours was going the other way."

"What did that do to your earnings?" I asked.

"Plenty. We'd been taking in sales and profits on the percent completed, and suddenly there were no buyers. Just costs. No sales, no profits, just lots and lots of costs. And some giant losses.

"It was like those cartoon pictures of Donald Duck when he runs off the cliff and keeps right on going as long as he doesn't look down and realize that he's out over the canyon. And then he finally does take one tiny look down, and *kazoom,* down he goes."

"You had some headaches in some other operations too, didn't you?"

"We had plenty of headaches, but the other really big

one was in the franchising operation where we had been selling operating territories and taking our payment in ten-year notes from the franchisees. Then the accountants decided they weren't going to let us consider those territory fees as regular sales unless we got paid in cash. That hurt us very bad because all those fees were pure profit for us, and when the accountants said we could only count a territory that was bought for cash as a sale, we got hit very hard."

"It sounds to me as though you were trying to work the accountants both ways—taking the construction into earnings piece by piece to get the reported profits from that as fast as possible and taking the franchise fees all at once to get the fastest reported profit from that, too."

"You bet. And I'd do the same thing any time. And don't let anybody give you a lot of sanctimonious crap about it either, because every time I did something like that I had lots of Establishment lawyers and accountants and brokers and analysts cheering me on. At least they did so long as I paid them their fees. Everybody wanted to go with me."

"What about the employees?"

"Which ones? I took some guys and paid them twice the salaries they'd ever had before. And gave them bonuses. And stock options. And a good time too."

"But the options were worthless, weren't they?"

"Only later on. They might have become rich men, you know. Millionaires, some of 'em. It didn't work out that way, but they knew they were taking some risks to have a chance to go all the way. And they got that chance. Never forget that. They got their chance."

"And the workers in the plant? What about all the men and women you laid off?"

"What about them? Sure, it's tough on the individual,

but is it better for the rank and file to keep too many people on the payroll and sap all the strength out of the company or is it better to run lean and have better pay and some real growth? You tell me. I'll take the lean and mean any day."

"You may be able to make it sound all-American to lay people off, but what about the times you used the assets of the employee pension fund to buy stock in companies you were trying to take over? And what about the big block of Western stock that you sold from the parent company to the pension fund when you knew the antitrust suit by the Government would make the stock collapse, and you stuck the pension fund with the loss?"

"All is fair in love and war. And business. Nobody would have complained if it had worked out. Nobody. And don't give me any sob-sister act about the middle-management guys who kept counting their stock options during the bull market and then went to the banks at the top of the market and borrowed a lot of dough to buy more stock. I'm not glad they went bankrupt when stock prices collapsed later on. Fact is, I'm sincerely sorry about that. But that was their lookout. I'm not my brother's keeper."

"Maybe not. But your own situation is lot different, isn't it?"

"You bet. I'm not ashamed of any part of it. My pappy always told me—and your pappy always told you too—look sharp and take care of Number One. And I did."

"You've worked out a series of management contracts with the parent company and each of the subsidiaries, haven't you?"

"Yes."

"How much are they worth to you?"

"Well, the total income to me each year on these management contracts is about $435,000. And they run until 1982."

"And what happens after 1982?"

"There's my pension and profit-sharing, which will give me about half that amount as long as I live. And I've got some deferred compensation to spread my '66 and '67 bonuses out over a few years. None of this is unusual, you know."

"What about tax shelter loans from the company?"

"I guess that is a little unusual. The way we worked it out, the company lends me and one or two other key executives enough dough so we can buy enough real estate so the depreciation of the real estate will offset our cash income. We repay the loans like a regular home mortgage with flat payments that include interest and debt retirement, and the payments are fully covered by the cash flow on the projects."

"In other words, you get your whole salary on a tax-free basis?" I asked somewhat incredulously.

"Yes, but it's a lot better than that because we are also building up a very substantial personal equity in those real estate projects using Uncle Sam's tax dollars and low-interest, long-term debt from the corporation. As they say in show biz, 'Can you top that?' "

"You're no longer working for the company, are you?"

"Not for four months, two weeks, one day and fourteen hours. But I'm still getting paid, buddy boy. I'm still getting paid. They've let go of me, but I won't let go of them. They still have to pay Numero Uno."

"As you look back, what would you say brought the company down? What was most important?"

"One thing. And only one thing. We lost control over

capital. Money is everything in big business, and we became big business because I could raise more money faster
than anybody else. We did so many complicated deals
so fast that none of those jerks at the banks and the Street
could keep up with us. And we always followed one
cardinal rule. No matter how much or how many different
kinds of Chinese money we might have involved in a
deal, the cold hard cash always, always flowed from them
to us. Always, always, always.

"We raised money with rights offerings, private place-
ments, converts, bank lines, commercial paper, take-overs
of asset-rich companies and every other way you can
think of. The key to all of it was our stock price. As long
as I could raise big money, we could 'buy' the earnings,
which would, in turn, keep the stock up."

"Everything was great as long as everything else was
great?"

"Yeah. So then when the accountants hit us with the
revision on franchise fees, the stock got hit bad and we
had to postpone a special subordinated convertible we
had planned to sell. That was the first time we had not
been able to take money from the market. Then the stock
market started into a big bear slide and we couldn't go
that route any more. And *then* the damned banks and
mortgage lenders tightened up on us and strangled our
whole real estate operation. We knew we were in trouble,
but we thought we might just scramble our way out of it.
At least until Hayden, Stone.

"I was so surprised when that thing blew. I don't think
I'll ever forget sitting in our 'War Room' when my secretary burst in with the news that Hayden, Stone was suspended and trading on the Big Board was halted. You
know the irony of it? She thought (knowing my feelings
about the Street) that I'd be really happy to hear about

it. She never even suspected that that bomb was going to blow up our company.

"The market drop that morning—in just ten minutes of trading—was enough to scare the banks into calling me for more dough. They were scared of the American stock, which they had been holding as collateral on our take-over loan. I guess they were right to be scared. It wasn't very good collateral, really. But Jesus Christ, they knew we didn't have any cash just sitting around. They knew we had just postponed our convertible offering. But they were in a panic."

"The president of the bank called right after lunch and said he had a bank examiner sitting in his office demanding they liquidate my loan by selling off the American stock. I couldn't believe this was happening. I told him there was no way he'd ever get that stock sold and he said something about having to pay the piper and I hung up.

"They tried to sell it Tuesday morning. Fat chance. In my own opinion, that dumb move is what really sealed the fate of Wall Street. They might have lived through Hayden, Stone but we and the banks hit them with a blockbuster from the blind side. I guess you could say we played the role of Samson in bringing down the temple." He fell silent, gazing vaguely into the dying fire.

"What are your plans for the future?"

"Oh, I'll probably just loaf for a couple more months. Take it easy for a while. The market's only beginning to put itself back together again."

"And then what will you do?"

"I'll do it all over again, of course."

"What?"

"Sure. That's my game. You're talking to the master. Don't you realize that? *Of course* I'll do it again."

"How, for goodness sake, are you going to get any

money? You've just driven a very big company into bankruptcy. You've lost a lot of people an awful lot of money. How can you ever dream of raising money in real size ever again?"

"But that's the point. I can do it any time I want to."

"But how?"

"Simple. So simple it makes me laugh. I won't have any trouble at all. First, I go to the banks and hock my future salary contract for a couple of million. Then we buy a division of a cash-poor company—maybe even from my old company. Then raise more dough in a private placement with some friendly, greedy institutions. We'll promise to double their money by going public later. Once we have a public vehicle, we can start doing deals and we're off and running once again."

"But why will they let you, of all people, get another chance? Why shouldn't they write you off as a bad mistake and refuse to play your game?"

"They won't because they can't. First of all, they're much too greedy. They just can't resist the chance to make a killing, and I'll give them a good shot at a big fat profit. Second, they think it will all be different this time. They can't remember and won't learn and don't really care. They all assume they'll get out first, and they all assume they'll have plenty of time to pass the crummy merchandise off on some other, bigger fool. They love guys like me the same way yokels love the pitchman at the carnival. It's so much fun to make believe that they fool themselves. Just like I said when we first started talking, Wall Street and Vegas have an awful lot in common. The big money goes to the entertainers and performers that attract crowds. I get big crowds."

"What will you call this new company?" I asked.

"Phoenix." He laughed. "Because it will literally rise from the ashes."

"What business will it be in?"

"Who cares?

"Nobody cares."

EPILOGUE

ALMOST EVERY firm in the investment field is encumbered by at least some of the major problems raised in this short book. The natural tendency in New York and Washington and elsewhere will be, indeed already has been, to minimize the seriousness of the situation.

The Exchange gratefully announced in the spring of 1971 that William McChesney Martin, former Chairman of the Federal Reserve Board, was making a broad-ranging study of the securities markets. When the results were published a few days ahead of schedule in early August of that year, virtually everyone in Wall Street sighed with relief because the report required no major changes in the Exchange or in members' business activities. The Exchange moved formally and deliberately toward the appointment of special committees to study the recommendations made by Mr. Martin. It was not without irony that Mr. Martin had made the last previous reform study of the Big Board, in 1938, after Richard Whitney, former President of the New York Stock Exchange, had been sentenced to serve a prison term in Sing Sing for feloniously using the securities of the customers of his firm for his own personal purposes. Times change, but slowly.

Men in high positions of responsibility counsel patience, moderation and caution in making changes in the stock exchanges. And perhaps they are right. But would they have been so measured in their reaction, and would we have accepted their moderation so calmly if Hayden, Stone had failed—as it so very nearly did on September 11, 1970—and if this failure had caused—as it might have —the failure in rapid succession of such major firms as Goodbody and F. I. duPont and Bache as well as other large but less well-known firms? How would the nation and the Congress have reacted to the great stock market crash that would have followed the failure of four of the five biggest brokers? Surely the Securities Act of 1973 would have been a major piece of reform legislation.

Of course it didn't happen. At least not quite. Mr. Golsen didn't say "No deal." He said, "O.K., Felix." A merger was arranged that September morning between Hayden, Stone and Cogan, Berlind, Weill & Levitt. And Merrill Lynch did agree in October to take over Goodbody (provided the Exchange membership agreed to indemnify it against the first $30 million of costs and losses it incurred). And a Texas computer magnate did take control of duPont, perhaps, in part, because it was an important customer of his high P/E company.

Slower trading volume allowed the members to catch up on fails, and record levels of underwritings brought in much-needed operating profits during the next eighteen months. And during 1971, as prices and volume recovered, lifting earnings, one major firm after another had a public offering of common stock. The crisis was passed with fewer than 200 firms failing or being forced to consolidate.

It is a fact that Hayden, Stone, Goodbody and duPont were rescued, but the truth is that *if* the rescue had not been achieved precisely when it was, Hayden, Stone would have been suspended from membership, and its failure would have forced other major firms to fail, thus precipitating an enormous stock market crash, a financial panic, and an international money crisis of a severity that has never been seen before.

The ultimate question is whether this nation should reform the securities markets only in response to what in fact did happen, or in response to what in truth very nearly happened, and could happen next year or the year after that or year after that.

Some readers will find this book outrageously harsh on Wall Streeters; others will see it as another piece of evidence that the problems in Wall Street are due to the reprehensible people in the business. I would not agree with either view. The system is not so much determined by the values of people as the values of the people are determined by the system. Although it deals only with the problem side of the Street, in no way is this book an indictment of the people in the Street (many of whom are my closest personal friends). It is, instead, a critique of the system, its deficiencies, and the ways in which the system might be changed fundamentally. I have discussed each of these reforms with many practicing investment professionals, and in every instance a majority agrees with the need for change in the specific area and accepts the validity of the change proposed here. Such fundamental change is much needed now.

Many readers, particularly those most prominently and intimately involved in the arcane complexities of Wall Street operations and traditions, will scoff at the reform program presented here, claiming that such radical changes simply couldn't be brought about without jeopardizing our nation's capital markets. They will find it far harder to make a strong case, based on either rigorous logic or factual data, to support their contentions that we should instead hold close to the *status quo*.

This book is intentionally limited to the opportunities for reform in the securities industry; it does not prescribe specific treatment for the problems arising from the ambitions and cavalier actions of corporate executives who delight in using Wall Street for their selfish purposes. Human nature is not going to be changed by legislation or by regulation, but the reformation of the securities industry proposed here could greatly reduce the incentives for Wall Streeters to go along with deceptive financial operators, and perhaps result in the eventual elimination of the financial wheeler-dealers who abuse Wall Street and the investing public.

Hopefully it will sufficiently dramatize the deeply rooted problems of Wall Street and the Exchange community that appropriate reforms will be enacted in the Securities Act of 1973. It took the 1929 crash to show the need to bring the exchanges up to date with the rapid emergence in the twenties of the individual investor and his needs. And it took the Bank Holiday to show the need for commercial banking reform. Now the exchanges need to be brought up to date with the needs of institutional investors. Modifications of the old way will not be sufficient; a new way is needed.

The Money Game is over. At least, it should be over.

Can't we as a nation deal with that reality without waiting for the ugly demonstration that could come with another crash? Can't the Second Crash be the one that never actually had to happen?